FROM BAD TO CURSE

A CURSED WITCH MYSTERY

ELLE ADAMS

1
___

Living in a castle had its perks. Aesthetics aside, it gave me the chance to live out my childhood fantasies of running down echoing corridors and commanding an imaginary army to conquer my foes. As a kid who'd grown up in foster care, I could be forgiven for wanting to live alone in the middle of nowhere with a big, fancy castle of my own.

One thing that was definitely not a perk—spiders. I evicted the latest unwelcome guest from my bedroom by catching it in a glass and throwing it out the window. Not my preferred method, but since magic was forbidden inside the tower, and the others would object if I conjured a flamethrower, I had to use what I had available.

That was unfortunate, really, because I could have sworn that the castle's spiders were finding ways to sneak back into my room on purpose. This was the fifth I'd found this morning alone. After closing the window, I tugged down a spiderweb dangling from the ceiling near the spot where it joined with the wall. If I had to guess, I would say they were coming from up in the attic.

If I dealt with the spiders at their source, it'd solve the problem, but that would involve setting foot in their territory. The idea was as appealing as gargling ectoplasm, but I'd fought monsters twice my size, and I'd never hear the end of it if my vampire housemate found out I'd let a few creatures smaller than my fingernails get the best of me.

A few creatures with eight limbs each. And eight eyes. Ugh.

Suppressing a shudder, I walked out of my room and then stared at the closed wooden door to the attic, trying to muster up the nerve to open it.

Footsteps sounded behind me. "Perry, are you okay?"

Tam, leader of our team, eyed me with a puzzled expression on his handsome face. What with his silky-smooth long hair, bright-green eyes, and tall, lean frame, I might have taken him for a vampire if I didn't know better. Despite being as fast and stealthy as a vamp, he didn't have the unfortunate blood-drinking habit or their nocturnal nature—the latter proven by the fact that we were both awake before everyone else in the tower. My brain short-circuited in an attempt to find an explanation that didn't make me sound like a wimp who couldn't handle a few harmless spiders. "Yes. I'm okay."

"You looked a little spaced out."

Heat crept up my neck. Had he caught me staring at him? "I'm trying to figure out how to spider-proof my room."

"Another one?"

"Five. I think they're coming from up there." I gestured at the attic door. "If there's a huge nest, I might need to visit the weapons room before I head up to face the carnage."

"Spiders aren't that bad. They kill flies."

"No flies would dare go near my room," I said. "Honestly, I'm doing the spiders a favour by kicking them out, but they don't seem to have got the message yet."

A hint of amusement entered his gaze. "I can't imagine they have. They don't tend to listen like people do."

"Some people don't listen either." I was a prime example myself, though I was trying to get better now I was part of a team. There was only one member who I clashed with on a regular basis, and I was thankful he was asleep. I didn't need the vampire to witness my ongoing battle with the castle's spiders.

Tam indicated the attic door. "I can come with you to check it out, if you like."

At his offer, my heart began to race. *Oh boy.* I'd been doing my level best to keep my attraction to him secret, so as not to jeopardise the trust developing between us as the team leader and the newbie, but at times like this, it was hard to ignore. Imagining being in the confined space of the attic alone with him sent heat rushing through me.

On the other hand, it would be kind of pathetic if I had to beg my team leader to get rid of the spiders when I'd gone head-to-head with an enraged demonic spirit less than a week ago. I had a reputation to uphold, after all.

"Never mind," I said, hoping he didn't see any signs of my internal struggle on my face. "I know a losing battle when I see one. I'll just get some bug spray or something."

"Fair enough." Tam moved towards the stairs. "I'm heading down to the office for a bit. I have an inkling Kellen's due to call in with our next assignment."

"I wondered when that would be." It hadn't been long since our last—first, technically—mission together as a team, but the Wardens made the word 'efficient' look like an understatement. As a team leader, Tam got some leeway in which missions we took on, though the orders always came from the main office. Specialist teams who dealt with magical monsters were in higher demand than one might think.

"We'll have to wait until everyone's awake to give them the details." He descended the wooden stairs to the floor below.

I took "everyone" to mean "Maurice." I'd already heard Callum and Farley heading downstairs earlier while I'd been engaged in a silent battle of wills with my unwelcome spidery visitors, but that was Tam for you. He always wanted to be fair to everyone, even towards our most antisocial member—aside from me, of course. One might have thought the two of us would have bonded over that commonality, but my history with vampires had mostly involved hauling them away in handcuffs, and to say I'd never had good experiences working with others in the past would be an understatement. Part of it was a personality issue, which I'd freely acknowledge. The other more signifi-cant part was the fact that I was cursed.

"Curse" is a loaded word in the magical world. The tamest curses were used to play practical jokes, such as ones that caused someone's hair to fall out or ants to show up in every pair of shoes someone owned. Nastier ones were slapped down with harsh punishments from the magical authorities, but the generic bad-luck curse placed upon me as an infant had flown under the radar until the first time I'd met the Warden's office's resident Seer. She'd fainted on the spot at the sight of me, and frankly, it was a miracle the Wardens had let me stick around after that debacle.

Granted, they could hardly throw a child out onto the street, even a cursed one, so they'd asked Kellen to keep an eye on me and kept me at arm's length from then on. I'd proven myself to the Wardens enough times that they'd had to accept me as one of them, though a bit of me suspected my habit of being shunted between offices in different cities was partly due to superstition on the office's part, as if curses were contagious. For the record, they weren't, but since curses could usually only be removed by the person who'd used them, and nobody knew who was responsible for mine, there was nothing to be done.

My phone began to buzz in my pocket as I followed Tam downstairs. After I'd fished it out, I found that Kellen was calling me. My supervisor—and the one who'd assigned me to this team—would likely be setting our next assignment, so I guessed he wanted to have a quick chat with me before-hand. Upon reaching the foot of the stairs, I answered the call. "Hey, Kellen."

"Perry," he said. "Got a moment?"

"Sure." I watched Tam descend the second staircase to the tower's lowest floor from my position on the landing, hearing the murmur of Farley's and Callum's voices from inside the living room. "I don't have anything going on, but I'm guessing you're calling because that's about to change."

"You know me well." I could imagine his green ogre's face crinkling in a smile. It'd only been a couple of days since I'd gone to his office and told him I'd be sticking with my new team. The news hadn't been a surprise to him, despite his taking a major gamble when he'd sent me here, but he'd known me for most of my life.

"So, what's the assignment?"

I entered the kitchen, noting with disgust that Maurice had left a couple of dead rats on the wooden medieval-style table. The vampire was worse than a stray cat.

"That would be telling."

I perched on one of the benches on either side of the table. "I thought that's why you called."

"Not exactly." His tone became more serious. "I just

wanted to let you know that this mission isn't going to be like your first one."

You don't say. It wasn't unheard of for him to give me a heads-up before difficult missions, despite his knowledge that I could handle pretty much anything, so I'd learned to humour him. Kellen had been the person who'd found me as a troubled child, and I owed him more than I could ever repay for getting me out of the regular human foster system. It had been hard enough being a witch living among humans, but when my curse was added in, it was a wonder I hadn't turned out completely dysfunctional.

"I gathered that we're going to be leaving Hexworth this time around," I said to him. "Right?"

"Not just that."

"Oh boy." Given the lead-up, I thought he was about to dump an unwelcome surprise on my head. "Go on. Give me the news. Is the mission going to involve spiders?"

"Not to my knowledge," he said. "No, the news is that the upper echelons of the Wardens have decided to turn the next mission into an opportunity to assess your entire team."

"What does that mean?" I asked. "Assess us in what way?"

"To evaluate how well you're working together ... that kind of thing."

My heart sank. "You mean they're sending one of their poxy inspectors to tail us throughout our next mission."

Great. I'd never got on well with the Wardens' higher-ups—authority figures generally brought out my rebellious instincts—but having to deal with one of their inspectors when my relationship with my new team wasn't quite settled yet was an obstacle I hadn't seen coming. We'd come a long way in the aftermath of our first case being resolved, but the last thing we needed was a third party stepping in and making things difficult for all of us.

One didn't argue with the upper echelons of the Wardens, though. Even I knew that.

"Sorry," Kellen said. "Not my idea. The inspector was already in the area you're being sent to, so it was an obvious choice for them to ask him to assess you."

Assessments were nobody's idea of a good time, but a certain vampire had better be on his best behaviour if we had to impress the head office.

"I'm sure it'll be fine," Kellen said. "Just wanted to give you a heads-up so you can let the others know."

"Cheers."

This was going to go over well.

"WE'RE BEING ASSESSED?" Maurice asked. "Seriously?"

As it turned out, Kellen's plan had been to phone Tam right after our call, at which point Tam had called a meeting for the entire team and forgone his plan to let Maurice sleep in. Normally, the living room was my favourite room in the tower, packed with cosy armchairs clustered around the fireplace, but the fire had yet to warm up, and a chill seeped through the cold stone walls. Living in a castle that had been built in the twelfth century did have a few downsides, spiders aside, but I couldn't deny it discomfited me a little to think of our next mission removing us from our base.

"We are," Tam confirmed in response to the vampire's question.

Maurice, the singular reason I was a little concerned that our team might fail the assessment before it even started, lounged in his seat with the elegance only a vampire could achieve. His pale face, as usual, was twisted in a scowl. "Just what we need."

"It's not that unusual," Callum said in his soft Scottish accent, attempting to calm the prickly vampire down. The laid-back werewolf was Maurice's polar opposite, which made it doubly surprising that they managed to live together without ending up as mortal enemies, let alone developing an amicable rapport. "It's been a while since our last assessment."

At his side, Farley lowered her head, her curly dark hair falling to either side of her face. "Yeah ... that was before we were down a member."

Oh. Right. My predecessor, who'd been a witch like Farley and me, had died in a tragic accident the previous year. The others didn't yet know that Kellen had told me the details, and I was careful to avoid thinking too deeply about the subject while I was around Maurice. The vampire claimed to have stopped using his ability to read my inmost thoughts without my permission, but I didn't want to take the risk.

"True," Tam said. "It makes sense that they'd want to check everything's going smoothly in here. I don't like it either, but they're being insistent."

"Typical of them," said Callum. "At least we'll avoid any unpleasant surprises later down the line."

We'd better. It was understandable that the inspectors would want to check up on the team, but they might have given us the chance to get through more than a single assignment first.

"I wouldn't speak too soon. Unpleasant surprises are kind of our thing." Maurice shot a brief look in my direction, as if to remind me of how my curse was also prone to rebounding upon the people around me. Coming from a guy who lived on blood and dead rats, it didn't particularly bother me, though I had to wonder what an outsider would make of our team dynamic.

"So ... what's the assignment?" asked Farley.

All eyes turned expectantly towards Tam.

"Our assignment is a little unusual," he said. "A couple of tourists were found dead near a small community of paranormals who live by the sea. Their village is very small, only a dozen or so houses, and the details of their connection to the deaths are unclear."

"We're staying with them?" asked Callum.

"No, they don't have anywhere for tourists to stay, so the Wardens had to pick a nearby village as a base," said Tam. "They found one within walking distance where paranormals can live openly, which also happens to be where the inspector is staying."

"Lucky us," Maurice muttered.

"How long will we leave the tower for?" Farley asked.

I'd been wondering the same thing. I hadn't lived in the castle long enough to establish a new routine yet, and we'd spent the couple of days since our last mission playing Cluedo: Paranormal Edition or watching horror movies on the massive TV that sat next to the fireplace. I wouldn't lie— I was going to miss the relative span of peace, however appealing it might be to have a change of scenery. While part of me relished the challenge of potentially fighting another monster, the prospect of dealing with an inspector was far less welcome.

"That depends on how long it takes for us to find the cause of the tourists' deaths," said Tam. "The local police department are stumped, but the details were suspicious enough to draw the attention of the Wardens."

"You think it's another monster that's attacking tourists," I surmised. "Right?"

"Correct," he answered. "As to what kind of creature it is … you know as much as I do."

"And in our line of work, anything is possible," said Callum. "Even another possessed tree."

"Pretty unlikely on the coast," I commented. "Possessed seaweed, perhaps."

"That actually sounds kinda horrifying," Farley said.

Whatever form our target took, it was our job as Wardens to remove the threat and ensure the safety of the surrounding humans, magical or otherwise. The Wardens had a reputation in the magical world as mostly being devoted to joyless paperwork over action, but that couldn't be further from the truth. Except for people like Kellen who worked in the offices, but the weirdo actually *enjoyed* that kind of thing, and I had no doubt that this inspector would be the same.

"Is the inspector involved in the investigation?" I asked. "Will they be helping or just observing?"

"Yeah, are they going to be breathing down our necks for the entire mission?" asked Maurice. "Or are we allowed to do our own thing?"

"I'll check," said Tam, "but I get the impression we'll be left to do the actual investigating alone. Certainly, the reason the Wardens called in a team is because they need our specific skills."

Thought so. Unlike the inspector, we were more suited to the monster-hunting part of the job than the paperwork, so it made sense for an independent team to be assigned to hunt down the beast who'd killed those tourists. Provided we had the freedom to do our jobs without being tailed everywhere we went by someone who was likely to be as much of a pain in the neck as a vampire's bite, then I'd go with it.

"Meaning they need us to hunt the monster while they put their feet up in their hotel room," Maurice said. "Gotcha."

"Hey, I'm not complaining," I said. "Will we report back to the inspector whenever we have something to share, and they'll leave us alone the rest of the time?"

"No, they'll want to interview the team members too." Tam looked at me. "Especially the newest recruit."

Oh, wonderful.

2

———

Maurice glared at Tam. "I am not letting her cast a spell on me."

So much for our mission getting off to a smooth start.

Tam had wasted no time in instructing us to gather on the gravel path outside the tower's squat grey walls, but getting to our destination was another matter entirely. The tricky thing about having a team of assorted paranormals was that not everyone could use the same means of transport, and Maurice had refused point-blank to let the rest of us ride in his fancy car. That meant he'd have to suck it up and let me give him a helping hand.

"Don't be difficult," said Callum. "Perry will use the transportation spell on all of us at once, so we'll land in the same place without any problems."

"Yeah, right. Knowing her, she'll drop me in the middle of the ocean."

"Well, now you've given me ideas." I rolled my eyes at him. "Honestly. Isn't it easier than flying? Or walking?"

The persistent drizzle in the air formed a thin mist that

suggested flying to our destination on a broomstick would be a risky move. In fairness, I might have also felt jumpy if I had to put my personal safety in the hands of someone who I'd spent most of the past week arguing with, but if he was going to be like this for the entirety of the mission, then we'd have a hard job convincing the inspector that we were an effective team.

"No," he said. "Actually, walking is no bother at all. In fact, I might do just that."

That figured. "Do you even know the way?"

"No," Tam interjected. "I told you we're travelling together. I don't want us separating before we even reach our destination, especially if the inspector is going to be waiting for us when we arrive."

True, and the last thing we needed was for Maurice's stubbornness to land the entire team in hot water before the mission even got off the ground.

"Exactly," said Farley. "I'd offer to use the transportation spell myself, but I haven't cast that charm since I was at school. I have a higher chance of accidentally dropping our entire group in the middle of the ocean than Perry does."

"I'll pass," said Callum. "I'd rather avoid going for a swim in freezing water, thanks."

"Agreed," Tam said. "Everyone packed warm clothes, right?"

"Yes." I wore a thick jumper underneath my coat, having learned the hard way about the average temperature up here near the Scottish border even in summer, but the sea breeze off the coast was reportedly even colder. I hoped we could wrap this case up quickly, and not just because of our upcoming assessment.

Maurice scowled. "I refuse to believe this is our only option."

"It's that or get on a broomstick," I told the vampire. "I can't promise I'm used to steering a broom in a gale, though. Fair warning."

"Same here," added Farley. "I haven't ridden a broomstick since I crashed into a tree when I was ten."

"You've made your point," Maurice ground out.

"Then there's no contest," said Tam. "We'll go with Perry."

Tam could move as fast as a vampire, as I'd seen for myself, but I remained in the dark as to his paranormal status. Yes, my usual method when I had the burning desire to know something was to ask straight out, but this was different. Aside from not wanting to jeopardise the tentative trust we'd established over the past few days, I'd be a hypocrite to judge him for keeping secrets when I had so many of my own.

"Fine." The vampire dropped his gaze. "Get it over with."

"Thanks for the cooperation." I put on a sunny smile and faced the rest of the group. "Ready?"

Farley, who I knew got jumpy whenever someone pulled out a wand without warning, nodded enthusiastically. "More than ready."

Getting out my wand, I pictured the destination in my mind's eye. Tam had shown me a picture of a wind-swept village nestled between sand dunes on the coast, and I focused on that image as I cast the spell. It wouldn't be quite as accurate as travelling to a place I'd been to myself, but I aimed to get as close as possible to the destination.

In a flash, the gravel path vanished, and a beach replaced it—or what passed for a beach in England anyway. The sand was mostly gravel, draped in seaweed and littered with large rocks.

"What have you done?"

I rotated on my heel towards the vampire's irate tone. Maurice stood several metres away, seawater swirling up to his ankles.

"Oops," I said. "Didn't realise the tide would be partway in."

"You did that on purpose!" Maurice said accusingly.

"I didn't." Transportation spells were only as precise as the user's knowledge of the destination, and I'd been going off a photo and nothing else. It was lucky we hadn't ended up further out at sea, really. "Could be worse. At least you don't have to swim to shore."

Instead of answering, he waded out of the sea and glided past, his feet spraying me with seawater and wet sand in the process. *Vampires.*

I turned towards Tam and the others. "Seriously. I didn't know we were even going to end up on a beach. I was picturing the sand dunes."

"I know." Tam rotated on the spot, the sea breeze ruffling his hair, and pointed out a sandy, grass-covered slope. "The village is this way."

My boots squelched in the wet sand, gravel crunching under my heels, and the sea breeze carried the smell of salt water. Maurice had already glided to the top of the sand dunes, leaving the rest of us to climb up the slow way. I let Farley and Callum overtake me and fell into step with Tam.

"You don't really think I dropped him in the sea on purpose, do you?" I asked him.

"No, of course not. I know it's hard to control where a transportation spell takes you."

"You'd think he'd know better." Unless the vampire had thought my subconscious had somehow guided the spell to dump him into the sea, which I was fairly sure wasn't even a thing.

"It's been a few years since he's used that spell, I expect," said Tam.

True. There were many perks to being a vampire, but when a witch or wizard underwent the transformation, they surrendered most of their magical abilities in exchange for immortality. The trade-off was supposedly worth it but not in the rare case in which one needed a wand. I doubted he'd have enjoyed flying on a broomstick with me either, so he'd have to deal with it.

Maurice got a little indirect payback when we reached the sand dunes. He'd glided effortlessly uphill, but my shoes sank into the deep sand to the ankles, and the tall grass was too sharp to go barefoot. Farley talked Callum into giving her a piggyback, but I had too much dignity to ask Tam to do the same for me, so I waded up the slope and ignored both the gritty sand in my shoes and the smirking vampire's presence at the top of the hill.

"Here we are." Tam pointed towards the grey-looking cluster of houses, which appeared to be smaller than Hexworth and was marked with a crooked sign that read Welcome to Herring Cove.

The name was appropriate enough, given that the smell of freshly caught fish filled the cobbled streets. Tam led us straight to the village's single bed and breakfast for travellers —which we'd be sharing with the inspector, now I thought about it—and I shook sand off my shoes before following him through the creaky wooden door.

A stern-looking woman greeted us on the other side, grey-haired and dressed in a frayed apron covered in old stains. "New guests, are you?"

"I'm Tam, and this is my team."

"It's about time you showed up." A man stepped out in front of the woman, cutting off her reply. Dressed in a waistcoat with a lot of shiny buttons, he was a head shorter than me and about ten years older. His smooth hair looked as if he'd ironed it flat, which was some achievement with the aggressive ocean wind outside. This had to be our esteemed inspector.

"I assume you're Inspector Peterson," said Tam, ignoring the man's impolite greeting. "I'm Tam, and this is Callum, Farley, Maurice, and Perry." As he spoke, he pointed us out one at a time.

"Which is the new one?"

The new one? I might have forgiven him for forgetting my name, but my hackles went up at being singled out already, let alone referred to as if I weren't a person.

"Perry?" Tam indicated me again. "That's her."

"That's me," I agreed.

The inspector scrutinised me as if I were one of the spiders I'd evicted from my room at the tower. "I'm told you have quite the reputation among the Wardens."

Uh-huh. Aloud, I responded with a noncommittal grunt.

"Yes," he went on. "I'd appreciate you speaking to me alone. A private interview, just between the two of us."

"What? Now?"

"Of course."

We had a monster to find, and he wanted to waste time with unnecessary interviews? *He has got to be joking.*

Tam stepped in. "What about the rest of us?"

"Oh, you can settle into your rooms." He waved a dismissive hand. "We won't be long."

We'd better not be.

Maurice shot me a scathing look as if to warn me against badmouthing him, while Farley's mouth turned down in a frown, and even Callum didn't look thrilled. It seemed we had to put off the investigation until I'd answered the inspector's questions satisfactorily, so I resigned myself to holding everyone up.

While Tam asked the inn's owner for the keys to the team's dormitories, Inspector Peterson led me towards a wooden door to the left-hand side of the reception desk. Based on the absence of anyone else, it looked as if we were going to be the only guests here. *Us and the inspector. How cosy.*

Another thought hit me. There was no way an inn of this size would have enough rooms for all of us. Would we have to share? *Please, no.*

"In here." The inspector beckoned me through the door into a room which contained a few tables and chairs and presumably served as the breakfast part of the bed and breakfast. He sat down at a table, and I took a seat opposite him.

"Perry," he said. "Peregrine Jacobs, is it?"

"Yes, it is."

He pulled out a notebook and a pen and placed them on the table. "You joined the team recently, correct?"

"Less than two weeks ago, yes." Which he knew perfectly well already, having seen my records. My foot twitched under the table, and I hoped he couldn't see my knees jiggling with impatience.

Pen in hand, he began taking notes. "This is your first team?"

"Yes." Again, this ought to be obvious to him. Had he not read my records beforehand, or was *he* being assessed on his own ability to ask annoying questions? "Kellen, my supervisor, made the call. If you've spoken to him, I assume you know the details."

"Ah, but I want to hear them from you." He paused in the middle of writing. "Your supervisor made an interesting choice in recommending you to this particular team, given your predecessor."

My predecessor? He must mean Clarice, the witch who'd died a year or so prior to my arrival in the castle. I didn't know much about her, only that she'd been an expert monster hunter who'd been possessed by the demonic spirit the team had been hunting and had died in a fire the demon had started in an attempt to kill the rest of the team. Tam and the others didn't know I was aware of the details, but I hadn't wanted to stir up bad memories by admitting I'd asked Kellen to give me the full story.

With great difficulty, I remained quiet until the inspector spoke again. "You're known among the Wardens for being a loner and not working well with others."

That's nice. I said nothing, since he hadn't asked a question, though I had to wonder if he'd called me in here to insult me instead of conducting an interview.

"Clarice was close to the rest of the team," he went on. "I gather you had a rough start, by contrast."

I raised a brow. "What would give you that idea?"

None of the mishaps of the past week and a half had been included in our reports. Tam had made sure of it.

He tilted his head. "I gather you called Kellen and requested him to reconsider appointing you to your new team immediately upon your arrival at the castle."

Ack. He must have pressed Kellen for my reaction to the news, and my supervisor would have had no choice but to admit the truth. "I wasn't prepared, so it was a surprise to find myself assigned to a team. I decided to try to make the best of the situation and to decide whether to stay after our first mission. I imagine you can guess what choice I made."

"Your first mission," he said. "A challenging one, I gather. Your team leader has dealt with tough situations beforehand, but I was interested to see you played a strong role in solving the case."

"We worked together." Was I supposed to take a back seat instead? "Everyone did their part."

Even Maurice had, in the end, but we hadn't mentioned our various wrong turns in the report we'd handed over to the Wardens' office, such as the times I'd accused the wrong culprit or Maurice's bright idea to try summoning the monster into the attic without asking the rest of us first. Either the inspector suspected there was more to the story than we'd let on, or he had a different agenda.

"So it would seem." He looked up from his notetaking again, while I tried and failed to read his scribblings upside-down. "How do you get along with the rest of the team? Tam, for instance, had a history almost as turbulent as yours prior to becoming a team leader. Has it been a challenge for you to submit to his authority?"

What was that supposed to mean? "Yes, it's fine. It's clear he knows what he's doing."

Over my dead body would I so much as hint at the crush I'd started to develop on him. I knew from experience that it was better to let my feelings run their course and fade out in time. I didn't do relationships, and I certainly didn't want to ruin our hard-won trust.

All the same ... what did the inspector mean by *turbulent history*? I'd thought Tam had joined the Wardens as a teenager and ascended straight to the position of leader. I'd rather eat sand than ask this dude for the details, so I'd have to think on that one later.

"I see," he said. "He and Clarice were particularly close, so I wondered if you might find it hard to settle into the team as her replacement. I'm glad to hear you worked out your troubles."

He sounded the opposite of glad, but my own thoughts were in freefall. *They were close. Did he mean to imply what I think he did?*

"We did." Whatever his agenda, I'd had about enough of this conversation. "We have another case to solve now, and I'd like to make some progress on it before the end of the day. Is there anything you wanted to ask me that isn't already in your records?"

His mouth tightened. I'd known that would annoy him, but it was clear that he was questioning me for purposes that had nothing to do with helping any of us with the case.

"It's important that we get a realistic impression of how you're fitting in," he said. "Kellen told me a little, but his position is a little ... biased, given your history. The rest of the team hasn't been assessed in a while either. I'm sure it seems immaterial to you, but it's essential to the Wardens for us to keep up-to-date records."

Sure it is. "I understand, but it's been a long journey. I'd appreciate the chance to clean up before we start our work on the case."

It'd hardly been a strenuous walk, but I wanted to get the sand out of my shoes and check on the room situation almost as much as I wanted to get away from the inspector. *Please say I won't be roommates with him.*

"Of course," he said. "If you want to talk to me about anything, then I'll be staying just down the corridor from your dormitory."

That wouldn't be happening. "Thanks."

At least he'd confirmed we weren't bunking in the same room. Leaving him behind, I strode back into the entryway and climbed the stairs to an equally narrow corridor. Three doors lined one side, and a small bathroom was visible through a fourth.

"In here," Farley called from behind the door at the far end of the corridor. "This is the girls' dorm."

I ducked into the room, which was small and cramped. Two beds stood inches apart, and the smell of damp permeated the walls. Not a patch on the tower, but I'd seen worse. I dropped my rucksack next to the unoccupied bed. "I was worried we'd all be crammed into the same dorm together."

"Luckily, no. Callum snores."

"And Maurice is prone to night-time wandering." He slept during the day, usually, but I doubted he'd want to stay behind with only the inspector for company while the rest of us went out investigating. I was relieved to spot a tiny bathroom at the side of the room. "Good, we don't have to share the facilities with the inspector."

"What's he like?"

The curiosity in her question made me pause. I knew I couldn't tell her he'd brought up my predecessor. They'd been friends, according to Kellen, and I didn't need to cast a pall over an already-grim situation. With luck, he wouldn't mention it to the others. *I hope.*

"Annoying. He asked me a long list of questions that he could have found the answers to by reading my files."

"Oh, one of those." She rummaged in her backpack, pulled out a bottle of water, and took a sip. "At least I'm forewarned when it's my turn to be interviewed."

"I got the impression I'm the one he's most interested in." I kicked off my shoes and peeled off my socks before heading for the bathroom to clean the sand off my feet.

"You know we're going straight back through the sand dunes again when we visit Grim Crag, right?" Farley called to me.

"When we visit *what?*" I backtracked to my rucksack and

rummaged inside for a pair of spare socks. "Grim Crag? Is that the place where the tourists' bodies were found?"

"You've got it," she said. "It's a village up on the cliffs. Name's a bit on the nose, but I think it's a coincidence."

"We'll see about that." I sat down on the mattress—or rather, sank into it—and began shaking the sand out of my shoes. I missed my room at the tower already, spiders and all.

Once I'd put on a clean pair of socks, Farley and I went downstairs to find the others. Despite the cold and the fishy smell, it was a relief to escape the stuffy room and feel as if we were making progress.

"Let's get a move on," said Maurice. "Unless anyone has any more unnecessary distractions."

As if it were my *fault the inspector waylaid me.* "Definitely not. Are we going to talk to the people who found the bodies?"

"I thought we'd drop by the local police office first," Tam said. "They have the details on the tourists' deaths. Afterwards, we can walk straight to Grim Crag and talk to the villagers."

"Good," Maurice grumbled. "No more wasting time."

"I concur."

It was past time to find out what had really happened out there.

3

———

The local police station was more of a shack than anything, consisting of a dingy room occupied by two unimpressed-looking officers who listened with a disinterested air as Tam explained what we were doing in Herring Cove. The rest of us crowded uncomfortably around the creaky wooden desk, which was littered with papers and weighted down with a hefty computer monitor that looked as if it'd time-travelled here from the 1980s.

"Two tourists died, I'm told," Tam said to the officers. "I'd appreciate it if you could tell me exactly what happened to them."

"That's right," replied the first officer, a grey-haired man whose name badge read Phil Sr. "A couple of hikers went missing the other night. Their bodies showed up in the water near the community of Grim Crag."

I found it difficult to believe a place with a name like that had never experienced any weird or creepy incidents beforehand. Had the people who lived there never seen a horror movie?

"There's not much else to say," answered the second officer, a younger man with coffee stains on his uniform and a droopy brown moustache. His name badge read Phil Jr. *Father and son, then.* "We're the nearest police office in the region, so we got called up to the Crag to fetch the bodies." His tone suggested he thought it ought to be someone else's problem, not theirs.

"Where are the bodies now?" asked Tam.

"At the morgue in the nearest hospital," said the elder guy. "It's in the next town over."

Well, that was inconvenient. "Has anyone determined the cause of death?"

The younger officer eyed me. "Drowning, officially. But there were odd marks on the bodies. To tell you the truth, they looked like bite marks."

"I might've thought it was a shark attack if we got sharks in these waters," added his companion. "But we don't."

You don't say. A shark would have to be incredibly lost to wind up on England's frigid northern coast.

"How'd they get into the water to begin with, then?" asked Callum from behind me.

"Fell in?" The younger officer shrugged. "The cliffs are steep, and the paths can get slippery in the rain. We'll probably never know." His tone suggested he wasn't fussed either way.

"We came here to find the cause of their deaths," Tam said to them. "If you have any information that might help us, then we'd be grateful if you shared it with us."

"If you want to look at the bodies, call this number." The older man reached for a scrap of paper and scribbled a line of digits before handing it over to Tam. "Otherwise, I'd suggest you talk to the villagers at Grim Crag."

"All right," Tam said. "I assume you've spoken to Mr Peterson?"

The younger officer grunted. "He's had no luck finding monsters around here. Maybe you'll do better."

Hmm. The inspector's job was to assess us, not to find the monster himself, but the officer's lack of optimism didn't help my own dimming mood in the slightest.

"If you see him, can you let him know that we're going to talk to the villagers of Grim Crag?" asked Tam. "We'll head there right away."

Phil Sr grunted. "Be my guest."

On that promising note, we left the shack-like building and found that it had started to rain. I pulled up my hood, which the wind pushed straight back down again.

"Doesn't sound like they've made much of an effort to find whoever killed those tourists," I remarked to the others. "You'd think it'd be bad for business."

"I think they stopped investigating when the Wardens got involved," Tam said. "Everyone okay with walking to the Crag now?"

"Did they name the place themselves?" I asked.

"Actually, yes," he said. "According to the information the Wardens gave me, anyway."

Herring Cove was unnerving enough in itself, frankly, though that might be the aftermath of the inspector's questions. Thanks to his references to my predecessor, I felt like we'd already run into a ghost before we'd even started the investigation.

Naturally, the inspector himself materialised as soon as we turned away from the police station. So much for leaving the village without being waylaid again.

"You've spoken to the police, then," he said, addressing Tam. "Good. What did they tell you?"

Tam gave Inspector Peterson a quick rundown of our chat with the officers while the rest of us stood and got rained on. When he'd finished, Tam reached into his pocket and pulled out the scrap of paper the officer had given him. "The police told me that the bodies of the victims are at the hospital in the next town over. While we're gone, I wondered if you might give them a call and ask if they have any more information to add. I suspect they might accept your authority over ours."

When the inspector's jaw twitched in obvious annoyance, I suppressed a smirk. I didn't know if Tam was right about the hospital staff being more likely to accept his authority, but if anyone deserved to trek all the way over to the neighbouring town to look at a pair of corpses, it was the inspector. And he'd be out from under our feet for a bit.

"I will speak to them," he said. "If they allow other visitors, then I'll let you know."

"I don't see him bothering to pay them a visit in person," I whispered to the others when the inspector departed in the opposite direction.

"I didn't think he would, but it was worth a try," Tam murmured. "That way we wouldn't have to make the trek ourselves."

"Or use another transportation spell," I added.

"Not a chance," Maurice growled.

"I thought you might object."

Tam led the way through the village's centre. The place was easy enough to navigate, though its size had obvious downsides—the nearest hospital being in another town, for one. There was a chance the bodies of the tourists might turn up a few clues, but I figured Tam wanted to ensure we didn't waste any time on detours when we had a limited number of hours of daylight in which to go monster hunting. Odds were we'd have better luck talking to the villagers than examining the bodies.

The road became a sandy path, which we followed westward until the sand dunes gave way to harsh cliffs. With the ocean breeze driving cold drizzle into my face, I buried my hands in my pockets and fantasised about the warm fire back at the tower. Maurice looked entirely too amused at my discomfort, but it was all right for him. Unlike the rest of us, vampires couldn't feel the cold. Granted, only Farley appeared to be as annoyed as me, while Tam seemed unbothered by the weather, and nothing dampened Callum's mood. Farley grumbled under her breath as she walked, and when she nearly slipped, Callum moved to walk on her right-hand side, his tall, muscular frame shielding her from the worst of the wind.

"These two hikers weren't exactly on a regular hiking trail," I remarked, shoving a handful of damp hair out of my eyes. "There's not even any scenery to speak of."

"We don't know whereabouts they were actually hiking when they vanished," Tam said. "They were last seen in a village some distance from Herring Cove, but the bodies washed up all the way up near the crags."

"You don't really think they fell into the water by accident, do you?" I asked. "And got bitten to death by fish?"

"No, but we can't be sure whether they were attacked on the land or in the water," he said. "Chances are they were killed elsewhere, and their bodies were pushed out to sea to hide the evidence."

I raised a brow. "You think the people up at Grim Crag might have had a hand in their deaths?"

"They found the body," he said. "I hope they'll be open to answering questions."

"I'm sure they'll be thrilled when we march in and

accuse them of murder," Maurice said under his breath. "Which I'm sure one of us is planning."

He expected me to try my usual blunt approach. Personally, I thought the direct approach was often the quickest route to answers, and I doubted he'd complain if we got to the bottom of these murders as quickly as possible.

"That's not the plan," Callum said. "Do the police or the higher-up Wardens genuinely think that someone from the village itself committed murder?"

"I doubt the police are fussed either way," Farley put in. "As for the Wardens, they called us out here for a reason."

"We're almost there." Tam pointed towards a couple of stone houses visible in the thin mist clinging to the clifftops.

"That isn't a village," said Farley. "It's barely even a road."

I counted twelve buildings at most, all clustered close enough to the cliffs that it was a wonder they hadn't been swept away by an errant wave. The cliffs jutted outwards over sharp-looking rocks that suggested anyone foolish enough to dive into the sea would have a rough landing.

"I'm guessing that's where the bodies were found."

I heard a faint barking noise, scanned the clifftop for the source, and spotted a woman wearing a pink waterproof coat with the hood pulled up. She was walking a bedraggled-looking poodle.

The woman came ambling over to our group. "Who're you?"

"Hello, there." Tam spoke first. "We're helping to investigate the deaths of those two tourists whose bodies washed up near your community. We wondered if it would be possible for us talk to someone who witnessed the event."

The woman gave us a distrustful look. "All of you are investigating, are you? You're not local."

"We're staying in Herring Cove," said Tam. "Is it okay if we have a look around?"

I'd wondered if the size of our group might cause friction with the locals. And it was hard to conduct a stealthy mission with five people involved, especially in a small community like this. Even the woman's dog was whining as if it wanted us gone, straining at its lead.

The woman gave us a long, scrutinising look and then grudgingly pointed towards a figure standing on the cliff's edge, his fishing line extending all the way out into the water.

"Fenton found the bodies," she said. "Don't expect to hear anything useful from him, though."

Without elaborating, she walked away, her poodle shuffling after her. Tam watched her leave and then approached the man she'd pointed out. He stood inches from the cliff's edge, his frail body swaying in the breeze and making me wonder how he'd kept his balance. Even Maurice avoided stepping too close to the edge of the cliffs, despite his vampiric abilities gifting him with the grace and balance of a professional dancer. Vampires weren't big fans of water, though, and I knew better than to tease him, given that I was more likely to trip and fall than he was.

The man with the fishing rod didn't appear to even notice he had company. He watched the sea intently, wearing a dressing gown and slippers, which struck me as odd, especially given the weather conditions.

Tam cleared his throat. "Excuse me?"

"I'm fishing," Fenton said without turning around.

"We noticed," I said. "You can talk and fish at the same time, can't you?"

"We wanted to ask a couple of questions," said Tam. "If that's okay with you, that is."

"Depends what they are." He continued to focus intently on his fishing line.

Undeterred, Tam pressed on. "We're looking into the tragic deaths of a couple of tourists near your village. I'm told you found the bodies."

"Yes, I did."

"And?" Tam went on. "Can you tell us anything about them?"

"They were dead."

I could see why the poodle lady had assumed we wouldn't have much luck questioning him. "How? The official reports say they drowned, but they had bite marks on their bodies, didn't they?"

"Aye," he said. "Sad, but that's how it goes sometimes."

"What do you think bit them?" Tam pressed. "Did the marks look like they belonged to an animal?"

"Dunno," he replied. "Not a marine biologist, am I? A fish is a fish, in my book."

"Neither am I, but most fish don't have sharp teeth, do they?" I pointed out. "Have you seen anything odd in the water?"

"Like what?"

Honestly. He seemed utterly oblivious to our actual need to get answers. That, or he was purposefully trying to annoy us into leaving, which was a distinct possibility.

"Like a monster." I opted to skip straight to the point. "A magical beast. You're a wizard, right?"

"Nah, I'm a dud. Always been better at fishing than casting spells."

Callum cleared his throat. "You'd know a magical beast if you saw one, right? Like, say, a kelpie?"

He nearly dropped his fishing rod. "There's a kelpie?"

"No, that was just an example," said Tam. "You really

haven't seen any unusual animals out at sea? Anything new that you've never seen before?"

"No, can't say I have. The fish are still biting, which is all that counts, isn't it?"

"If you say so." Given the notable absence of any fish in the bucket next to him on the clifftop, it didn't look as if he'd caught anything today, except perhaps a chill.

"What about people?" asked Callum. "Seen any strangers in the area?"

"Yes," he said. "You."

Farley made an irritated noise. "Aside from us, that is."

"And the victims," Tam added. "Before the two tourists' bodies showed up, did you see anyone new in the area? In your village or outside it?"

"No. There's nobody new here," he said. "The coven won't let just anyone sign up."

"Coven?" I echoed. "Are they in charge here?"

"That's right. Scarlet's coven."

"Who's Scarlet?"

"The village's leader," Tam said out of the corner of his mouth. "Elected by the people, according to the information I got from the office."

"You didn't mention that earlier." I kept my voice low, though Fenton was paying too much attention to his fishing line to notice our whispering.

"I hoped we might find the information we needed without having to talk to her," he muttered. "Sounds like I was right to believe they aren't interested in speaking to outsiders."

"Maybe we should have gone to the next town over to look at the bodies instead." We might as well have questioned the poodle lady instead, for all the use this guy had been. "Sent the inspector in our place."

"That wouldn't have been wise." Tam turned back to address Fenton again. "If you haven't seen anyone new in the village itself, what about nearby? Don't people come walking in the area?"

"Tourists come and go all the time," he said. "I don't pay too much attention. The fish're all I care about."

Hmm. If he was right, and the monster that had killed the tourists hadn't been in the water, then it was possible the culprit wasn't in this small community at all, and the bodies had washed up here by sheer chance. But the deaths had snagged the Wardens' attention for a reason, and we had to narrow down the location somehow.

"There don't seem to be that many tourists," Tam commented. "I imagine your fellow villagers know one another well enough that you'd be aware if someone here knew something about the deaths that they hadn't told the rest of you. Is that correct?"

"Nobody here gives a damn about tourists." He remained focused intently on the sea. "We look out for each other, no more."

He hadn't answered the question, though that wasn't necessarily a red flag in and of itself. I glanced at Farley, wondering if her ability to sense emotions might have picked up on anything amiss. In fact, Maurice could read his *thoughts*, so if Fenton had been hiding any knowledge he hadn't shared, there was a fair chance that our vampire already knew. I couldn't read *his* mind, though, so I'd have to wait until later to ask.

Fenton let out a sudden yelp. The fishing line jerked in his hand, and he began to bounce up and down on the balls of his feet in excitement.

"I caught one!" he crowed, tugging on the line. "I caught one!"

The rest of us watched as he reeled the line in from the water. A shoe dangled from the other end, waterlogged and covered in seaweed.

"That's not a fish," I told him.

He didn't answer, continuing to reel in his fishing line. When the shoe reached his hand, he plucked it off the end of the line, and, as we watched in bewilderment, he took off the pair of slippers he was wearing and put the shoe on his left foot.

"I lost this weeks ago," he told us. "Now I need to find the other one."

A baffled silence spread through our group, and even Maurice looked utterly nonplussed at the half-barefoot fisherman's apparent delight.

Callum spoke first. "Is that what happened to the rest of your clothes?"

"Funny you should say that—"

Farley cleared her throat. "Guys, we have company."

We followed her line of sight, where several other people approached the cliff. The woman with the poodle was among them, accompanied by several others who wore long cloaks and carried wands. Most were female. *Witches, then.*

A cloaked woman with blazing-red hair strode to the front of the group. She had to be Scarlet, the leader of the coven who ran Grim Crag and the person in charge of the village.

And she did not look happy to see us.

4

———

The newcomers halted in front of us, their group fanning outwards to block our route back from the cliffs. As our team's empath, Farley would have felt their anger before she'd even seen them, but I didn't need to have the same ability to sense the hostility pouring from their group in waves. Their faces were as hard as stone, and they might as well have been waving pitchforks at us.

I briefly hoped Fenton might come to our aid, but he was back to casting his line out to sea, presumably with the intention of finding his other missing shoe—or the rest of his clothes.

Tam strode out to meet the newcomers, displaying no fear. "Hello. I'm sorry to intrude, but we're—"

"With the police. We know," said Scarlet. I could only assume she'd acquired her name *after* she'd dyed her hair, given that its vibrant shade of red couldn't be her natural hair colour. "We already spoke to them."

"We're not with them," Tam said. "We're members of the Wardens."

"Sounds like the police to me," said the woman with the poodle. "We've had enough of them coming here and hassling us."

"They came here because people died." As per usual, my mouth decided to speak before I could think better of it. "Sorry if the dead bodies were an inconvenience to you."

The tension in the air thickened as everyone's attention zeroed in on me, especially Scarlet's. I knew I shouldn't have started by insulting her, but she was acting as if we'd committed a mortal insult just by being here. It wasn't as if we'd knocked on anyone's doors or otherwise intruded on their privacy, so there was no need for the woman with the poodle to have gathered Scarlet and her minions to confront us.

"We're not here to impose on anyone," Tam added. "As the two tourists' bodies were found near your village, we wanted to ask if you've seen anything unusual in the area."

"Such as what?" Scarlet enquired. "That sounds more like an excuse for the police to start poking their noses into our business."

"They don't seem all that interested in you." Yet again, my mouth took the lead without my brain's permission. "We, on the other hand, are interested in getting rid of whatever magical monster attacked those tourists. We won't interfere in your business unless you have something to hide."

"You most certainly will not," said the witch. "Besides, if two normals got themselves caught in a storm and drowned, it's not our problem."

"Is that what you think happened?" I glanced at Maurice, whose jaw twitched, but he didn't otherwise indicate whether her thoughts contradicted her words. "You don't think they were attacked?"

"If there *was* a magical threat in the area, we'd take care of it ourselves," she said. "Now, get out."

The coven members closed in at her command, blocking off all the roads except the way back along the cliffs. Maurice shot me a glare, no doubt irked at me for losing my temper, but the attitudes of the villagers suggested that this venture had been doomed from the start.

Tam gave a nod. "We're not here to cause strife, so if you'd rather we leave, we'll do so right away."

"Go on, then." Scarlet watched, her arms crossed, while we walked across the clifftop until we left the cluster of houses behind us. The others gradually peeled away from her and returned to their homes, but the woman herself remained, her bright hair the only splash of colour against the gloom, until she vanished from sight behind the houses.

"Great one," Maurice snarled at me. "That's how you ruin a job."

"Did they look like they were going to help us in any way?" I raised a brow at him. "They'd already made up their minds, I guarantee."

"Yes, they had," Farley put in. "They were following that Scarlet woman's lead, and she was as hostile as a rabid manticore. If we'd stayed a moment longer, they might have tossed us into the sea to join those tourists."

"Exactly," I said. "I'm not in the least bit interested in negotiating with someone like that. I was already on the brink of throwing that Fenton dude's fishing rod into the sea. He was as much help as a plastic wand."

Farley snorted. "Yeah, I'm not going to complain about not being in range of their bad feelings anymore. Guess it makes sense that a community as small as this one would rally around a coven leader, unfriendly or not."

Personally, I'd have used the word *cult* instead of *coven*. I opened my mouth to ask Maurice if he'd read anything from their thoughts, too, but Tam came to a sudden halt, and then Farley did too.

"Someone's following us." She spun on her heel, and the rest of us followed suit as a man stepped onto the path behind us.

At first glance, the newcomer looked a bit like a Viking, given his long, tangled straw-coloured hair and his thick fur coat and boots. "I couldn't help but overhear your little altercation with Scarlet."

"You and the rest of the village," Maurice said sourly.

"Sorry about them," he said. "If you wanted to talk to someone, then I don't mind answering a few questions. I'm Walter."

It would have been more use if he'd offered his help earlier, though we'd still have been outnumbered by the rest of the coven. Would he end up in trouble with Scarlet if she found out he'd followed us? He looked capable of holding his own, given the wand in his belt, but it sounded as if everyone would have had to submit to Scarlet's authority in order to be allowed to stay in the village.

"Do you know anything about those two tourists whose bodies washed up near your village, then?" asked Tam.

"Afraid not," he said. "I know the bodies showed up on the rocks down at the beach. Scarlet had to call the police."

"Bet she loved that," I muttered. "I'm surprised she didn't just dump them back into the sea."

If she'd voluntarily called the police, then it was unlikely she'd been responsible for the murders herself. But we couldn't strike Grim Crag off the list until we knew for certain that nobody in the small community had been involved in the murders—perhaps not even then, if the inspector objected. I wondered if *he'd* been up here.

Walter glanced at me. "Scarlet's protective of her fellow villagers, but it's with good reason. Most of us don't fit in with regular people. Some less so than others. We take care of each other."

"Regardless, we have a job to do before we can leave," Tam said. "Have you seen anything odd in the area?"

"I'm afraid I don't leave the village much," he said. "I can't say I've noticed anything that would give me cause to worry, not until the bodies showed up."

Farley shifted on her feet, which made me wonder if she'd detected a lack of sincerity in his words, but she didn't speak.

"We spoke to Fenton first because we were told he was the one who found the bodies," Tam said. "But he didn't have anything to share that we hadn't already heard from the police."

"Ah, I wouldn't expect much from that one," he said. "He's a few planks short of a boat, he is."

"We wondered if he might have seen something out at sea," Tam explained. "I believe the tourists were attacked by a predator, and if it came from the sea, then it's as likely to present a threat to your community as anyone else. Our role as Wardens is to protect everyone."

"Wardens, eh." He gave Tam a considering look. "What makes you think the tourists were attacked? I thought they drowned."

"The bodies were covered with bite marks," Tam said. "We're specialists in dealing with magical beasts, so we were called in to help out. It's possible the attack took place on land, but even then, the beast responsible might be within reach of your village. Scarlet can't close her eyes to the truth."

"I see." Concern furrowed his brow. "What can I do to help?"

"Ask your fellow villagers if they've seen any suspicious signs," Tam said. "Magical beasts rarely go undetected. There'd be strange noises at night, maybe footprints..."

"Not that I know of," he said. "We'd know if there was a predator in the area. Scarlet might be distrusting of outsiders, but we're safer here than we would be elsewhere."

Tam paused for several moments before continuing. "I gather that she'd be displeased if we implied the threat might be inside her community itself, then?"

"You would be correct." He spoke in gravelly tones, his gaze shifting towards the houses. "Scarlet would never entertain the possibility."

Tam studied his face. "Has anyone in the village been acting strangely?"

"They have, haven't they?" The words came from Farley, whose shoulders were tensed. "There's something ... worrying you."

His brows rose. "You're perceptive, aren't you? Am I correct in guessing you're a Seer?"

"Close. Empath." She folded her arms across her chest. "You're hiding something."

"It's nothing, really... You must know, we don't typically gossip about our fellow villagers behind their backs."

"It's not gossiping if it might save lives," Farley pressed. "If it's bothering you that much, it's worth mentioning."

He exhaled a sigh. "I'd ask you not to tell Scarlet I told you this, but I suppose that isn't likely to be a problem."

"Told us what?" I asked, instantly suspicious. "What is it?"

"See that house there?" He pointed towards one of the

cottages near the end of the cluster. "The woman who lives there has recently turned into something of a recluse. She often takes walks outside at night when nobody else is around, but otherwise, we rarely see her. She used to be an active participant in coven meetings, which is why it strikes me as odd, but Scarlet has never brought up her absence. Alana, she's called."

"I assume she wasn't with the others who chased us off?" I asked warily.

"No, she wasn't. Like I said, she keeps to herself." His tone sounded as if he disapproved of that choice.

"All right," Tam said. "We'll speak to her. Thanks for letting us know."

"I'm glad I could be of assistance." He gave our group a last searching look before departing, his wild hair blowing sideways in the wind.

"Might it be worth speaking to this woman?" asked Callum.

"I think so," Tam said slowly. "If she isn't close to Scarlet, she isn't as likely to be hostile towards us as the others were."

"Until we tell her one of her fellow villagers thinks she's up to no good," added Maurice.

"*Was* he telling the truth?" I wasn't the mind reader, so I couldn't be sure, but Farley's reaction alone suggested Walter had approached us for reasons other than the desire to help. "The full truth?"

Maurice simply turned away without answering my question, while Tam frowned at both of us. "I'll do the talking. There might be an innocent reason this woman has started taking night-time walks, but most magical beasts are nocturnal. She's more likely than the others to have seen something amiss."

"Agreed," said Callum. "Might as well try all our options."

Not that we have many. Scarlet had long since disappeared amid the houses, but that didn't make me any keener to approach the village again. Tam took the lead, scanning the surrounding area to make sure no other villagers were waiting to ambush us, while Maurice lagged behind, which was unusual, since he could outpace the rest of us with ease, but against my better instincts, I fell into step with him.

"Maurice," I said, "did you pick up on anything when you read that Walter guy's mind?"

"Why would you assume I read his mind?"

"Because you always do." He'd told me himself that anyone who wasn't on the team was fair game, and it was the quickest way to judge someone's trustworthiness. "That's not an insult, Maurice. We need to know if he's leading us astray."

He shrugged. "Find out for yourself."

To my consternation, he quickened his pace and glided far ahead of me, making it quite clear that he didn't want to talk any longer. I hadn't expected him to get so defensive over a simple question, especially one that made perfect sense for our current situation. Why would he suddenly care about people's privacy? He'd had no qualms about delving into anyone's mind beforehand, including mine.

I caught up to Callum and whispered, "What's his problem?"

"I have no idea," he murmured back. "You're right—it *would* help if we knew how sincere that guy was. And the others, too, come to that."

"Exactly," I said. "You'd think he'd have at least tried."

"He probably did." He lifted his gaze to watch Tam,

who'd slowed his pace a little when he saw Maurice. "I'll ask him later when he's calmed down."

It would have been nice if we'd known whether Walter had been sincere when he pointed us in Alana's direction. Though he'd at least given us a lead, which was more than I could say for anyone else we'd spoken to.

I caught Farley's eye, and she gave the faintest nod. "What? Sure, the guy was pretty on edge, but my empath abilities can't tell *why* people feel what they do."

"I know," I said. "Just thinking on his intentions on pointing us towards this Alana person. We don't need to step into the middle of someone's personal grudge."

"That's not our biggest issue." She slowed her pace. "The villagers are really riled up. That much, I can tell."

"Is Scarlet still outside?" I cast a glance in Tam's direction, but he continued onward without stopping. "I don't see her."

"No, but I bet she's scheming with her coven on how to drive us off in case we try to come back," said Farley.

Maurice walked close to Tam, while I racked my mind for reasons that the vampire might have taken issue with my question and came up empty-handed. He wasn't jealous again, surely.

Tam came to a halt. "Farley, Callum, stay here, and keep an eye out for trouble. Maurice, circle the village, and make sure no one else is near enough to overhear us. I want to be sure nobody will sneak up on us while we're talking to Alana."

Farley nodded, her mouth pressing into a thin line. I wasn't even an empath, and the villagers' anger had got under my skin, so I could only imagine how much worse she had it—Maurice too. Being inundated with the villagers' hostile thoughts wouldn't have done his mood any favours, but whatever was going on with him, I couldn't afford to let it distract me.

At Tam's instructions, Maurice departed around the village's outskirts, while Callum and Farley waited at the end of the road, leaving me to approach the witch's cottage with Tam.

"You want me to come with you?" I asked, somewhat surprised that he trusted me not to run my mouth again. That, or he *didn't* trust me not to get into a fight with any coven member I ran into—which I had to admit was a distinct possibility.

"I think two of us would be less intimidating than our entire group showing up on her doorstep." Tam came to a halt in front of the cottage and knocked on the door. Nobody answered.

The curtains were drawn in the windows without any gaps, preventing me from seeing if anyone was inside, but Tam knocked again. This time we heard a distinct thud from behind the door, followed by a scraping noise. After a minute, the door swung inward, revealing a tall woman who wore a hooded cloak that covered her body from head to toe. "So, you're the ones who've been causing all the trouble."

5

———

On the other side of the door, Alana peered up at us from underneath her hood. She was younger than I'd thought at first glance, since her stooped posture and long cloak made her look like an old crone rather than a young woman with a pretty heart-shaped face and silky dark hair that surely hadn't seen the fierce wind outside. If she'd been walking around wearing that cloak at night, it was no wonder that Walter had grown suspicious of her.

"Trouble?" Tam echoed. "We're not causing trouble."

"Sounded like it to me," Alana said. "You brought Scarlet marching out into the street with half her coven, didn't you?"

"All we did was come to ask a few questions," Tam said. "We're with the Wardens, but Scarlet's coven seemed to think we were working for the police."

"Well, that'd explain it. Not a fan of outside authority, Scarlet isn't."

"We noticed," Tam said dryly. "I'll level with you—we'd rather not cause any more of a disturbance than we already have, but we're investigating the deaths of a couple of tourists whose bodies washed up near your community. All we wanted to know is whether anyone here has information that might help us to identify the cause."

"I don't know anything about that." Suspicion glittered in her eyes. "Why'd you come to me, then? Who sent you here?"

"Another villager mentioned you'd been walking outside at night recently," he said.

"Who told you that?" she asked indignantly. "Busybodies."

I weighed the odds and then said, "The guy told us you weren't part of Scarlet's inner circle, so we hoped you'd be willing to talk to us."

"We already spoke to Fenton," added Tam. "The other villagers were less receptive to our questions."

"I'm not surprised." She eyed Tam then me. "You came here in a big group? No wonder the others felt threatened."

A murmur of voices arose from further down the row of houses, and I tensed, as did Tam. His manner remained calm as he addressed Alana in a low voice. "We didn't expect this level of opposition to our arrival. We're staying in Herring Cove, and our supervisor requested that we speak to the villagers who found the bodies. If we had any other leads, we wouldn't all need to be here."

"I expect not." She grimaced and backed into her house. "Fine, you can come in."

Tam and I followed her inside. The downstairs room smelled of a witch's brew, which was an improvement on the ever-present stench of fresh fish which seemed to permeate the entire region. Two chairs and a sofa occupied the living room, all of which were ancient enough to appear on the verge of collapse.

"Right." The armchair creaked when she sat down. "What did you want to know?"

"Have you seen anything odd during your night-time walks?" Tam didn't sit down, though the sofa didn't look sturdy enough to hold one person, let alone two. "I'm guessing that since you invited us in, you do have something to share."

"I invited you in so Scarlet wouldn't toss you all into the sea."

"She's welcome to try." Tam spoke in light tones that didn't quite hide the steel beneath. While he didn't carry any visible weapons, I doubted he'd left the inn without the stick-like instrument he always brought with him on monster-hunting missions.

"I suppose you can handle yourselves, can't you?" She gave him a considering look then turned to me. "And who's this one?"

"Perry," I answered. "I'm here to help find whatever attacked those tourists. The bodies had bite marks on them. They didn't drown."

"*Bite* marks?" She blanched. "I didn't see the bodies myself, so I assumed the reports were true. It's not unheard of for the occasional tragic accident to happen on the coast."

"This was no accident," Tam said. "You understand why we need to know if you've seen anything unusual in the area."

"I have... You know, I *did* see a large creature near the sand dunes a few nights ago. I thought it might be a shifter, but it was big and furred, and it didn't look much like a werewolf. Granted, I was too far off to see it clearly, but I'm almost positive there was a *person* walking behind it."

"A human?" I queried.

"Sure looked like one to me," she said. "That's why I

thought it must be a shifter and their friend, but we don't get shifters of that size around here. I can tell you that much. Not many shifters at all, in fact. They don't like the cold."

"How close to the creature was the person?" asked Tam. "Close enough for it to have seen them?"

"Without a doubt."

"Near the dunes... You mean near Herring Cove?" Unease slid down my spine. "Why were you that far from home?"

"I like to go for a wander at night, when the weather's decent," she said. "Didn't expect to run into another person at that hour, let alone one with such an unusual pet."

"Pet?" I asked. "That's what you think it was?"

"That or something escaped from a zoo." She shrugged, her hood slipping a little to reveal more of her pale forehead. "No, it was too close to human habitation not to be trained to leave them alone."

"And you didn't recognise the person?" Tam queried.

"No," she said. "Like I said, it was dark, and I didn't want to get too close to that thing, frankly."

"Understandable," said Tam. "We appreciate you letting us know."

"Might be nothing," she said. "I tend to mind my own business, you understand, and I assumed my fellow villagers were the same."

"Most are." Whatever Walter's motives in sending us here, at least we had another potential lead. "We'll check it out."

"You'd better make sure Scarlet isn't waiting to ambush you outside."

I'd had the same thought. Tam approached the door and opened it a fraction to peer out into the street. "All clear. Let's find the others."

"Best of luck," Alana called after us as we left the house.

"What do you think?" I asked Tam when I'd closed the door behind us. "Was she being honest?"

"As far as I could tell, yes."

That wasn't the same as having the confirmation of a mind reader, but until Maurice got over his temper tantrum, it would have to do. "A mysterious creature near the sand dunes has to be worth checking out."

"What creature?" Farley overheard us from the street's end, where she and Callum waited. "Found us a monster to hunt down?"

"Alana seemed to think the monster in question was someone's pet." I filled them in while we waited for Maurice, but the vampire didn't materialise.

"Weird," Callum said when I'd finished. "Yeah. I can't say shifters would be fans of this climate."

"She wasn't specific on the size, other than 'bigger than the average shifter,'" I said. "Which is pretty big." Werewolves were larger than their wild-animal counterparts but not as big as, say, an elephant or a lion.

Farley paced in circles, shivering. "Where's Maurice?"

"Good question," I said through chattering teeth. "Might he have gone back to the inn?"

"I'd like to do the same," Callum ventured. "It's bloody freezing out here."

Typical. If I had to guess, I would say Maurice wanted to avoid me ambushing him with more questions, but it would have been nice if he'd told us he was going rather than leaving us to wait in the cold. I might have said he'd been purposefully trying to hold us back if I hadn't clashed with him over a similar situation during our first mission and turned out to be mistaken about his motives. But that didn't make his refusal to share important information any less annoying.

"We can walk back and wait for him to catch us up," I suggested. "He can lap us blindfolded, so there's no need for us to slow down."

"True." Farley moved into the lead. "Can't say I'm keen to get back to the inspector, though."

"Nor me." I buried my hands in my pockets. "You know, Alana said she saw the strange creature near the sand dunes. Might be worth looking around on the way back."

"Might be." Callum sounded ill at ease. "Wasn't the inspector supposed to be here on a mission himself?"

"Was he?" I looked between the others, my gaze landing on Tam. "Wait, didn't the police mention something about him not having much luck finding monsters?"

"He was certainly here on a mission for the Wardens before he was assigned to us, but I don't know the details," he said. "We'll have to ask him."

"You think he'll tell us?" Farley asked sceptically. "He'll probably say it's above our pay level."

"If he was looking for the same monster that attacked the tourists, then he'll have to tell us." I tugged my coat tighter around myself as we walked, but the cold air sought out every gap. "Not that I'm holding out much hope. He seemed more interested in interrogating me on stuff he might easily have read from my file. Hazards of being the newbie on the team, I suppose."

"Rather you than me," Farley said.

"I wouldn't speak too soon," Tam said. "It wouldn't surprise me if he wanted to have a private chat with every one of us at some point or other. This is a team assessment, after all."

"Is that why Maurice did a runner, do you think?" I looked at Callum, who shrugged.

"I've no idea," he said. "He usually annoys the inspectors to no end because he keeps voicing their questions aloud before they have the chance to ask them."

"And he criticises *me* for not playing by the rules." I gave an eye-roll. "Whatever the inspector was originally here to do, this case is still our job. I'd say we should have a look around the dunes before he ensnares us in another inter-rogation."

"You're not wrong." Callum pulled up the hood of his coat as the wind blew drizzle into our faces. "I don't know how the people here can stand being so close to the cliffs. You'd think they'd be concerned a storm might sweep the whole lot of them into the water."

"I don't know how they can stand the smell of fish," I said. "I won't be able to look at a cod after this without picturing Fenton and his shoe."

"Ha." Farley bounded into the lead as the sand dunes came into view. "Whereabouts did Alana mention seeing the mysterious monster again?"

"Around here somewhere."

The village's signpost lay ahead of us on the right, while on the left, the sand dunes sloped downward to the gravelly beach. I resigned myself to having my shoes inundated with sand throughout the rest of the trip and waded into the grass along with the others.

"Are you sure the victims weren't stabbed to death with one of these?" I snapped off a long strand of grass and held it up in demonstration. "I bet you could slit someone's throat with this."

"Not everything has to be a weapon, Perry," said Farley.

"Anything can be a weapon, if you're creative enough." I

dropped the strand of grass and caught sight of an area that looked a lot flatter than the rest. "Hey … is that a footprint?"

"Or paw print?" Callum walked closer to the patch of grass, which certainly looked as if something large had stomped it flat. "I'd say it is."

Tam strode over to join him. "Yes … it's some kind of print."

"That too." Farley pointed at an imprint in the sand further downhill. "Something's been walking around here, and it wasn't that witch lady's poodle."

"Not a shifter either." Callum crouched beside the print and inhaled. "I might have been able to pick up the scent, if it wasn't so windy out here."

"There must be other prints," Tam said. "A trail leading back to where it came from."

"It didn't come from the water," I said. "Not if we believe Alana's account, anyway."

"Don't speak too soon." Callum pointed down to the beach, where more flattened grass levelled out into wet sand. Patches of gravel had been disturbed in such a way that suggested something with large paws had run across the beach.

We made our careful way downhill to check out the trail. On the wet sand, it was easier to make out the shape of each individual imprint, which resembled a large paw with blunted claws.

"Some of the prints lead into the water, and others lead away." Callum pointed at two distinct sets of footprints. "The creature came down here, but it didn't stick around."

"Might've gone for a midnight swim." I scanned the beach, the wind lashing my hair into my face and wet sand sucking at my shoes. "Smell anything?"

Callum sniffed and shook his head. "Nothing but salt

and sand. Let's follow the tracks leading away from the sea. If we're lucky, we might find its home on the other side."

"Good call."

Farley walked close behind him, while Tam kept an eye on the tracks as we walked back uphill. In the grass, it was hard to tell which prints led in which direction, but at the very top, Callum halted.

"Look." He pointed to the left, where the faint impression of a print was visible on the path that circled the village. "The creature was close to the houses. Really close."

"Oh boy," I murmured. "I *hope* it's just a harmless pet and not a deadly predator."

The clawed prints sure didn't look like they belonged to anything harmless, but when the sand became hard pavement, the prints ceased.

Callum shook his head. "End of the line."

"Want to knock on a few doors and ask if anyone has a monster in the basement?" Farley suggested. "I have a hard time believing nobody in the village is aware."

"Same here." But did the inspector? No Warden would let a monster go unwatched, surely. "I wonder what it is."

"We can make an educated guess based on the prints," Tam said. "I have my laptop with me, so I can access the Wardens' files, but we should take a few photos first."

"On it." I pulled out my phone and snapped some pictures of the prints at the edge of the sandy path. "I can send these to Kellen. If that doesn't work out, then our monster's owner might take it for another walk tonight."

"It'll be dark soon," Tam said, "but it's a risk, going after a monster without knowing what it is."

"I hope Maurice doesn't get ideas about going for a nocturnal wander alone," Callum remarked. "I know he does it all the time at the tower, but it's much riskier in an unfamiliar place like this, especially with predators in the area."

"I wonder where he is." His disappearance wasn't much of a surprise, but I hoped he'd show up before nightfall, if just so the inspector wouldn't have the impression that we couldn't keep track of our own teammates. "Might he have discovered a passion for fishing and joined Fenton?"

Callum snorted. "Am I the only person who's starting to find the smell of fish unbearable?"

"Definitely not," I said. "If they're serving fish at the inn tonight, I'll skip the main course."

"It's a fishing village," Farley reminded us. "Bet it's the only thing on the menu."

"Oh joy." A sweeping breeze rippled across the dunes. "I get why Maurice doesn't like this place, but he can join the club."

"Too right," said Farley. "This place is ... well, weird is an understatement."

"Not all that unusual in our line of work." In the course of my time as part of the magical world, I'd seen more than my fair share of weird, but there was a difference between the regular type of weirdness and the sort that the Wardens were called in to deal with—the sort that put curses on newborn children and caused tourists to wash ashore with bite marks on their bodies.

"I meant it's *creepy,*" she elaborated. "Not haunted, but it has the vibe of the sort of place where you could disappear and never be heard of again."

"I mean, it is called Grim Crag," I said. "If it were called Happy Cliff, we wouldn't be having this issue."

Farley snorted a laugh. "What now, then? You don't really want to go back to see the inspector, do you?"

"To start off with, I think we should let the police know

about those prints," Tam said. "Then we'll see the extent of the inspector's knowledge, though it's possible he took us up on our suggestion to go to the next town over and look at the bodies."

"Hope he did." Maybe we should have gone there, too, but our trip hadn't entirely been a waste of time. We'd learned several valuable clues, at least, including that the monster responsible for the tourists' deaths might be closer at hand than we'd realised. Not a pleasant prospect, but it would certainly make our lives easier if we were able to keep our investigation within the village of Herring Cove instead of tangling with Scarlet's coven again.

Unless that Alana woman lied when she mentioned seeing the monster, which is possible. Neither the empath nor the mind reader on our team had been present when we'd spoken to her, and while it was obvious from the footprints that something big and dangerous was in the area, that didn't make it responsible for the murders. We couldn't overlook the victims' proximity to Grim Crag altogether, especially given the coven's commitment to secrecy.

Finding the source of the footprints would be a starting point, and we'd go from there.

6

The police, naturally, were about as happy to see us as we were to see them.

"You're back," said Phil Sr. "Find anything?"

From his tone, I knew he didn't much care either way. Tam closed the door behind us as we struggled to spread out in the cramped office. As before, there was barely enough room for us even without Maurice here.

"Were you aware that there are the footprints of some kind of large beast outside the village?" asked Tam.

The younger officer, Phil Jr, grunted. "Footprints? You want to report footprints now?"

"Given the size of the prints, there's a fair chance they might belong to a predator that's dangerous to humans," said Tam. "We found a clear trail leading from the beach to the village."

"If a shifter wants to swim in the sea, it's not our business," said Phil Sr.

"It's not a shifter," I cut in. "The prints don't belong to anything I recognise, but we spoke to someone at Grim Crag who told us she saw a large beast near the village, bigger than a shifter. Considering two people recently showed up dead in the area, I'd take this seriously."

I hoped they'd leap into action right away, but the two officers exchanged sceptical glances.

"You've some nerve telling us how to do our jobs," said Phil Sr. "Footprints indeed. You've hardly been here a handful of hours, and you already think you know better than we do."

"It's *our* job to find the cause of those deaths." The impatience in Tam's tone surprised me, though I didn't blame him for being irritated with the officers. "I wouldn't have drawn your attention to those prints if it wasn't potentially urgent. If it's not too much of an inconvenience, I'd appreciate it if one of you came with me to look at them."

Ha. If you asked me, I'd say the officers were lucky the villagers hadn't swarmed into the office, demanding to know if they were going to deal with the monster, though the news of the tourists' deaths might not have reached everyone yet. I'd bet they'd have reacted differently if the victims had been from Herring Cove instead of a pair of tourists.

The two officers exchanged glances again, and the younger sighed. "This had better be worth it."

Phil Jr followed us outside into the street, where Tam led the way to the sandy path leading to the beach. Callum pointed out the creature's prints, and the officer peered down at the faint outline with an unimpressed expression on his face.

"What's that supposed to be?"

"Footprints," Callum said. "Not a shifter's. I *am* one, so I should know."

"That's a human print." The officer pointed to the faded outline of a boot.

"Those are ours," said Callum. "Look, you can see the

creature's prints leading both to and from the beach, and they definitely came back here to the village."

"And there's an inspector from the Wardens staying here," I reminded the officer. "So you might want to make it a priority."

"Him." The officer scowled. "The Inspector isn't here."

"Wait. He isn't?" I asked, disarmed. "Where is he, then? Did he go to the next town over to look at the bodies of those tourists?" I was surprised he'd bothered, though there wasn't much in the way of entertainment around here.

"Can't say I know," he said. "I'm going back to the office. Whatever those prints are, it's not my job to fight monsters. It's yours."

"And it's your job to protect the citizens of Herring Cove." I knew a losing battle when I saw one, but his attitude made me want to poke him until he did his job. "There's a chance the next victim will come from within the village itself. What'll you do then?"

I could sense Tam's disapproval, but the police needed to take this seriously if we wanted to stand a chance of finding the monster before it claimed any more victims. We couldn't do everything alone, and the officers were the ones who had the authority to arrest the monster's owner, if it had one.

The officer narrowed his eyes at me. "Then your people will be the ones to deal with the fallout, not me."

"No pressure, then," I murmured as he walked away. To Tam, I added, "What're the odds of us convincing the inspector to prod him into action?"

"Unlikely." His jaw twitched. "He's right. It's our job to fight monsters."

"Only if we know what we're looking for." I studied the nearest print. "Should I go ahead and send a photo of these to Kellen?"

"Sure." He watched as I pulled out my phone and sent the photos I'd taken to Kellen, asking him if he was able to identify what creature they belonged to.

"Do you think the inspector *is* at the local hospital?" I slid my phone back into my pocket. "Should we join him?"

"If we do, it'll be better if we have the whole team with us," said Tam. "We should go back to the inn and wait for Maurice."

Since the inspector wouldn't be waiting for us there, I resignedly gave in.

"There you are." The inn's stern-faced owner beckoned to Tam from behind the counter. "Will you all be staying here for dinner?"

"We will," Tam said. "Is your other guest around?"

"Yes, he's in there." She pointed at the door to the dining room, which Callum opened to reveal none other than Maurice himself sitting at a table, sipping from a flask. He must have intentionally avoided us on the way back, and it was a good job nobody else was eating, given the blood dribbling from the corner of his mouth. *Vampires.*

Tam's mouth parted. "I meant the inspector."

"He went out for a walk earlier. He isn't back yet." She turned away. "Dinner will be served in an hour."

She hadn't said whether he was at the hospital in the next town over or not, but Tam thanked her anyway.

"I'm going to fetch my laptop," he told the rest of us. "Wait for me in the dining room."

"He left his laptop in the dorm?" I whispered to Farley. "Risky."

"We're the only guests, remember?"

If I were Tam, I wouldn't trust the inspector not to go snooping through our files, though he'd have difficulty, if Tam's laptop was as secure as his office back at the tower.

Since we didn't have a designated room for team meetings, we'd have to risk being overheard by the staff at the inn as we gathered in the dining room.

Ignoring Maurice's leave-me-alone gaze, I sat down next to him. "We have a lead."

He grunted. "And?"

"I thought you'd want to know." I retrieved my phone from my pocket and opened my photos to show him the images of the prints. "When Tam and I spoke to Alana, she mentioned sighting a large beast near the sand dunes. On our way back, we found footprints leading down to the beach—and more, closer to the village."

He gave my phone screen a glance and followed it with a shrug. "Your point is?"

"My point is that either there's a predator hiding near the village, or someone has an interesting pet." I pocketed my phone again. "I'm inclined to believe the latter."

"Same." Callum sat down opposite me. "Either way, we're going to find out what it is. You want in?"

Maurice put down his flask. "By 'find out what it is,' you mean beat the crap out of it, right?"

"If necessary," I replied. "We don't know for sure that it's responsible for those tourists' deaths, but the police are disinterested, and the inspector's gone walkabout. Do you know if he's at the hospital?"

"I haven't the faintest idea," he said. "You don't know what the creature is, then?"

"Yet," I said. "I sent a photo of the prints to Kellen so he can check the records."

"Didn't that backfire on you before?" he asked. "In fact, I distinctly remember that the last time you pinned your hopes on a response from the office, the castle's power went out, and we ended up with no signal."

"Thanks for that." I still didn't know if the incident during our previous mission had been due to my curse or simply the weather, but I didn't appreciate his bringing it up. "This time it's not a possessed tree we're dealing with. We also got clearer photos of the prints."

"I'd have thought you'd be up for some monster hunting," said Farley, who'd sat down on Callum's other side. "Aren't you?"

"Only if it's an actual monster we're looking for," said Maurice. "And what're you planning to tell the inspector?"

"Nothing," I said. "Unless he comes back before we leave. In which case, we'll ask him for an update on the state of the bodies."

"Didn't the police already tell us?"

"Like I said. They're useless." I leaned back in my seat. "They don't care, especially now we're here. They think we're going to do their work for them."

"The inspector thinks the same." Maurice drank deeply from his flask of blood. "I'm not staying in here tonight while everyone's asleep. Just to be clear. I'm going out."

"Tell that to Tam, not me." It was a surprise that he'd admit he had night-time plans at all. Hoping it was a sign he was willing to talk, I asked, "Where've you been? Did you come back directly here from Grim Crag?"

"What do you think?" He put down the flask and wiped his mouth on the back of his sleeve, leaving a bloody trail. *Lovely.* "Where's Tam?"

"Here." Tam walked into the restaurant with his laptop under his arm and sat down at the end of the table. "I'll check those footprints against our records, though I'm sure Kellen will get back to you soon."

He opened the laptop and began browsing, while I traded theories on monsters that could be kept as pets with the others. Luck was with me for once, and within ten minutes, my phone buzzed with a message.

"What is it?" asked Callum, catching sight of the grin on my face as I read the text on the screen. "Good news?"

"I got a reply from Kellen," I said. "He says the prints are most likely a giant chimera's. That or a lion, but he said that's unlikely."

"A chimera?" Tam moved behind my chair to read the message on my phone screen. "Yes. Chimeras are usually formed of two or more creatures. Like a cross between a lion and an alligator."

"Lovely," said Callum. "They're not native to the UK either. Someone must have brought it here."

"Or it escaped from a magical zoo," I added. "Can they legally be kept as pets? Does anyone know?"

"I think you'd need a licence," said Farley, "but if it's untrained, they might end up in a tangle with the law."

"If it attacked someone, certainly," said Tam. "It's also clear that its owner has been taking it outside the village at night, so we have an opportunity to confront them in person."

"But we're not going to kill it?" Maurice sounded disappointed.

"If it's a pet, then no," said Tam. "Proving the creature was responsible for the deaths of those tourists needs to be our priority."

The vampire scoffed. "Next you'll say we need the inspector's permission."

"We probably do," I said. "Even if we aren't going to kill it, there's a chance it might put up a fight. Does anyone have experience with chimeras? I've fought one before, and it ended in several buildings going up in flames."

"Why am I not surprised?" asked Maurice.

"This one doesn't sound like the fire-breathing variety," said Tam. "Not if it likes to swim in the sea. I'd say an alligator-lion hybrid is more likely."

"Who cares what it's made of?" asked Maurice.

"I do because I'd like to know what we're up against," Callum said. "We're heading out tonight, then?"

"Yes," Tam said. "I think it's best that we nip this in the bud as soon as possible."

Darkness soon fell. At dinner, we endured an entirely disappointing meal of fried fish with the inn's owner and her scowling husband. The one upside was that the inspector remained absent.

"I don't blame him for finding a nicer restaurant," Farley remarked as we returned to our dormitories to prepare for the mission. "I'll be tasting fish for the next week."

"Same." I opened the door to the dormitory. "Do you think that's where he is?"

"That, or he went fishing, like you said," said Farley.

"I wonder if Fenton found his other shoe yet." I pulled two daggers out of my rucksack. That would do nicely. "Everyone here is mad."

"Speak for yourself." She shot me a grin across the room. "How many knives did you bring?"

"Enough." I hoped so, anyway, though I wondered at which point exactly Farley and I had become friendly enough to tease each other. As an empath, Farley took longer than most to adjust to meeting new people, but I could say the same for myself. It was a change from dealing with Maurice's surly attitude, and I found myself in good spirits as we headed downstairs to join the others.

Tam waited for us to gather outside the inn and then addressed the whole group. "Try not to make too much noise. We need to find the creature first, if possible."

The sound of someone clearing their throat from the shadows made my heart sink. *Oh no.* The inspector was back, and he didn't look particularly thrilled to see us leaving the inn. "Where are you going at this time of night? Do you have a lead on the attacks?"

"Possibly," said Tam. "We have reason to believe there's a chimera in the area."

The inspector's brow crinkled. "Is that a joke?"

"Certainly not," Tam said. "Why? Were you already aware of this beast?"

"Yes, I was, because it's why I was sent to this region in the first place," he growled. "I was told that there was a possible case of an unregistered chimera being kept as a pet."

"You know it's a pet?" As his attention swung towards me, I added, "There are footprints—I mean paw prints—near the beach. You were investigating *before* those two tourists were attacked?"

An ugly flush marked his face. "I told them to send backup sooner."

He was supposed to stop the creature from hurting anyone. A surge of annoyance hit me. He'd acted as if our presence here was a nuisance, but we'd been sent to do *his* job, despite his outranking us. The Wardens' office had some serious explaining to do ... and so did he.

"Do you think the chimera attacked the tourists?" asked Tam. "Because if it did, then the Wardens should have informed us from the start."

"The owner has an alibi, allegedly," he muttered. "You can talk to her for yourselves if you want to assuage your curiosity, but there's no proven link between the tourists' deaths and the creature's presence in the village."

"That doesn't sound like the Wardens," Tam murmured. "There's ... Maurice, stop!"

The vampire glided out of sight, covering the length of the street in a blink. I moved after him at a run, rounding a corner into the village's main street. There, the vampire had frozen, looking ahead as the shadow of a large creature came into view. Easily the height of a man, it had the shaggy mane of a lion, an alligator's tail ... and a collar around its neck.

A leash connected the collar to a squat woman with wild curly red hair, who startled at the sight of Maurice and me.

"Excuse me?" Tam said from my side, startling me almost as much as the creature had. Where had he come from?

The chimera growled at our group, pawing the ground.

"Simmer down, Cupcake." The woman stepped around the creature, holding the lead firmly in one hand.

"You called your monster *Cupcake*?" There was no feature of the giant lion-alligator that looked remotely like a bag of baked goods.

"He's not a monster," she said. "Is there a problem?"

"Do you have a licence for that thing?" She wasn't even trying to hide her questionable pet from the police or anyone else. "We found a chimera's footprints in the area and assumed a predator had moved in to feed on the villagers."

"Oh, you're with the... What're they called?" She snapped her fingers. "The Wardens. He called in backup? Really?"

"Yes, we're with the Wardens," said Tam. "You must be aware that chimeras aren't commonly kept as pets."

"I have a licence for him, as that inspector of yours knows well," she said. "I thought he was done here."

"He didn't tell us that," I said. "Listen, we're here to find whatever beast killed those two tourists whose bodies washed up near the crags. The only trail we found led us directly to you."

Her brows shot up. "The Wardens think Cupcake *killed* people?"

"If you let him outside unsupervised, then it's possible, isn't it?" Tam queried.

"No," she said. "I'm always with him, and he sleeps in his cage at night."

Hmm. She might have the bias of a pet owner, but despite its occasional growl, the chimera seemed tame enough and comfortable around its owner.

"Why do you walk him at night?" asked Tam.

"Because he's scared of people," she said. "I heard two tourists drowned, but I didn't hear any rumours about any beasts. Are you sure the coven in Grim Crag didn't take issue with them walking too close to their village?"

"What would make you say that?" asked Tam.

She adjusted her grip on the lead. "They're not keen on outsiders."

"We noticed," I said. "Have they attacked tourists in the past?"

"No," she said, "but there's a first time for everything."

Hmm. She might be well-informed on Scarlet's coven's hostility, but if I were her, I wouldn't want to admit my beloved pet might have committed a crime. I peered at the chimera's face, which resembled a lion's except with one obvious difference. "Does... Does he have any teeth?"

"No," she replied. "The poor thing had an accident as a baby and lost them all."

I frowned. "There were bite marks on the bodies..."

"Really?" Relief crept onto her face. "Not—Not that I

want to celebrate them being dead. That's bad, but it can't have been him. Cupcake, show your teeth."

Cupcake's toothless maw opened, and he drooled all over the road. I took a hasty step back to avoid being drenched for the third time in a day. *Yeah ... he didn't bite anyone.*

"Thank you for your time," Tam said to her. "We'll be going now."

"Wait. We will?" I glanced at the others, but Maurice had already disappeared, and Callum and Farley had remained outside the inn with the inspector without joining us. "All right."

Leaving the beast and its owner behind, we returned to the inn.

"I gather that you saw the beast for yourself," said Inspector Peterson. "Is your curiosity satisfied?"

"He doesn't have any teeth," I said. "You might have mentioned that."

"You never asked," he said. "That Lara woman bought him on the internet from a foreign trader, allegedly."

"She said she has a licence," said Tam. "Is that true?"

"The office is chasing it up," he said. "Checking the records. It takes time."

"She seemed to think you'd agreed to leave her alone." That didn't matter when we'd been chasing the wrong lead from the start. "Is there anything else you want to tell us? You aren't investigating any other magical beasts, are you?"

"No," he said. "I don't appreciate the accusatory tone, Peregrine Jacobs, especially given your team's obvious short-comings. Is it typical for you to approach dangerous beasts without consulting one another on strategies first?"

"We had strategies," Tam cut in. "It was clear from the instant we saw the lead that the beast was no wild beast, so we had to improvise. If the creature has no connection to the deaths we're here to investigate, then it's a good thing we didn't react first."

"Speaking of which, you just went to the hospital to look at the bodies, didn't you?" His comments on our strategies had stung, but I wasn't about to let him slip away without giving us the information we needed again.

"Yes, I did," he said. "You were correct in assuming my authority would outrank yours, and I was able to get a close look."

"And?" I tried to keep my voice free from impatience, without success. "They didn't drown, I take it?"

"That's the official story, according to the police," Tam added. "The officers said there were bite marks on their bodies."

"They didn't give you any more details?" he asked. "Such as what the bite marks belonged to?"

"I thought that's what we were called here to find out," I said. "Why? What *did* the bite marks look like they were left by?"

There was a long silence before the inspector replied, "A human."

7

―――――

I didn't expect to sleep well that night, but at some point, the drizzle turned into a raging storm that battered the windows of the dormitory. I tossed and turned, but my bed was hard and uncomfortable, and I could hear Callum snoring through the wall.

The thoughts of the murders didn't help matters either, especially the inspector's revelation that *human* teeth marks had been found on the bodies. The rest of us hadn't seen them for ourselves, but my brain wasted no time in ticking over the implications instead of letting me rest. If I had to admit it, though, I would say a fair amount of my unease came from not being in the tower. Despite having lived there for a comparatively short time, I'd grown used to my new room, spiders and all.

I dozed off for a few hours and woke to the sound of a door opening elsewhere in the corridor. Farley was fast asleep in the bed next to mine, stretched out on her back, but the sound of soft footfalls on the stairs reached my ears. Who was awake? Maurice certainly wouldn't be in bed, but he moved too stealthily for human ears to detect. With my curiosity officially piqued, I tugged on some clothes, moving quietly so as not to wake up Farley.

After sliding my feet into my boots—which were still damp and filled with grains of sand—I left the room. The doors to the other dorms were closed, but when I approached the stairs, I heard the unmistakeable thump of the front door bumping against its frame.

The rain pounding on the roof had ceased, but the cold breeze was as persistent as ever, creeping through gaps in the walls. I made my way downstairs and wasn't entirely surprised to open the door and find Tam standing outside.

"I expected you wouldn't be able to sleep either," he said quietly. "Given that you're an early riser."

"That, and my mattress is so bumpy it's like sleeping on a pile of rocks." I pulled my coat tighter around myself. "The storm kept me awake for hours. I bet that woman didn't take her pet chimera out for long last night."

"I can't imagine she did, no." He began to walk down the street, away from the inn. "Better not to wake up the others yet."

"Farley was out for the count, and so was Callum, from the sound of his snoring," I said. "Lucky them. I'm guessing Maurice isn't back from his nocturnal wanders yet."

Tam made a noncommittal noise in reply. Perhaps he didn't want to talk about the vampire behind his back, though the way our voices echoed in the silent street made me aware that we might not be the only people in the village who were awake.

Like the inspector. Since he was in a separate room to the rest of us, there was no way to tell if he was asleep or creeping around town, making a nuisance of himself, but I'd prefer to avoid another altercation with him at this hour of the morning. By mutual agreement, Tam and I followed the road out of the village to the sand dunes.

"I hope there haven't been any more attacks overnight," I murmured. "Though I doubt any hikers would have been outside in that weather."

"I hope you're right," Tam said in a low voice. "I'd be more concerned about the villagers at Grim Crag, though they must be used to rough weather."

"More than they are to outsiders, apparently," I remarked. "Are we going to talk to them again today? Because if we've ruled out the chimera as the culprit, then they're back on the hook as potential suspects."

"I never took them *off* the list, to be honest," said Tam. "Their attitude to outsiders aside, the coven struck me as the sort who would think nothing of covering for a murderer among their group."

"True." I heaved a sigh. "I really thought we'd solved this one when we found those prints. I should have known it was too good to be true."

"It was a good guess," he said. "Chimeras are dangerous, and I wouldn't have expected anyone to keep one as a pet. Or it to have no teeth."

"Maybe it has a sibling we don't know about," I suggested. "It wouldn't surprise me, given everything the inspector didn't tell us. It'd have been nice if the Wardens had clued us in on the reason he was sent here."

"It was on me to ask for the details," he said. "I should have, but I didn't realise there might be a connection between our case and his."

"He came here to deal with one magical monster and ran into another?" I arched a brow. "In our line of work, there's rarely such a thing as a coincidence."

Maybe we needed to give the chimera a second look, but

the sheer oddness of *human* teeth marks showing up on the dead bodies cast all my theories into doubt.

Tam's gaze drifted back to the village. "I'm debating whether to talk to the police again as soon as their office opens for the day. I suspect at least some of the communication difficulties are coming from their direction."

"I bet." Between them and the inspector, it was a wonder we'd made any headway at all, though I had to admit I was glad I'd come outside to get this quiet moment with Tam before all hell broke loose again.

I cast a sideways glance at him, wondering how he always seemed so put together no matter the circumstances. By contrast, the sea breeze had sapped all the moisture from my face, and my hair had tangled in a halo which probably made me look like a demented scarecrow. Tam's hair remained silky smooth and his features as perfect as a vampire's. *Not human,* a voice in the back of my brain reminded me, and my interview with the inspector had only birthed a thousand more questions. Had our mutual trust progressed to the point I could ask him straight out? That, I didn't know—yet.

He tilted his head, catching me looking at him. "Something on your mind?"

I chickened out. "The inspector. Why'd the office put him in charge of assessing us, if he's supposed to be here to deal with the chimera lady's licence and not the murders?"

"It's not that unusual," he said. "In fact, I expected something like this to happen. Maybe not this soon, but the Wardens usually send someone to conduct an assessment after a newcomer joins the team."

"I should have expected it too." Though that didn't explain Inspector Peterson's general attitude problem. Why did they have to pick someone who seemed to have an irrational grudge against me? Sure, plenty of the Wardens did, but I was willing to bet Kellen hadn't chosen him. "I wish he'd just let us get on with the job. That would make it easier."

"He will," said Tam. "I think we made a mistake in sending him to look at the bodies instead of going ourselves, though talking to the people of Grim Crag was beneficial to us as well."

"Would they have let us into the morgue?" I had my doubts, based on the inspector's comments the previous day. "It saved us time, and it's not like he had much else going on."

Aside from waiting for the Wardens' office to stop dragging their heels on wrapping up the dilemma over whether Lara had a chimera licence, that is. If I'd been in his place, I'd have made the murders a priority and actually helped our team rather than hindering us.

"True," said Tam. "It can't be fun for him to be stuck in a place like this for the duration."

"Let's hope our own stay is a short one." I shivered, burying my hands in my pockets. "I want this case wrapped up, but I think we all need to be on the same page for this to work. Have you spoken to Maurice since we got back?"

At his hesitation, I went on, "I wondered if he read anything from the minds of the people in Grim Crag or even here in Herring Cove. Do you know why he's so reticent to share?"

"Maurice can be ... difficult sometimes," he said. "But if there's anything he hasn't shared, it's usually for a good reason. He'd never jeopardise the mission."

The underlying tension beneath his words hinted that he hadn't forgotten Maurice and I had nearly split the team apart in our last major argument. I'd vowed not to let that happen again, whether we were reporting to an inspector or not, but did Maurice agree?

"I'm sure he wouldn't, but he's gone off and acted alone before, hasn't he?"

"So have you."

Guilty. "Not this time. I'm on my best behaviour."

Though it might explain some of my restlessness since our arrival in Herring Coven. While I'd accepted that I was part of a team now, the old instincts remained, and when one added in the presence of a none-too-helpful inspector, it was no wonder I felt like we weren't making any progress.

"I didn't mean to imply you weren't," Tam said. "If anything, we're all guilty of keeping our thoughts to ourselves sometimes."

Was he referring to his own secrets? Unbidden, my mind drifted back to the inspector's comments the previous day. While I'd been surprised that he'd implied Tam had had as turbulent a past as I had, it was what he'd said about Clarice, my predecessor, that had really got under my skin. Had she really been close to Tam? There was no way I could *ask* him that without it backfiring in my face, but the questions remained in the back of my mind.

After several moments of silence, Tam said, "Let's head back and see if any of the others are up."

As it turned out, they were—with the exception of Maurice, who, Callum informed us at breakfast, was sound asleep in the dormitory.

"He must have sneaked back in when you were out," Callum told me over an unappetising meal of cold scrambled eggs. *Better than fish but not much.* "Where'd you two go?"

"For a walk," Tam answered. "I considered paying the

police a visit when their office opens, but I decided against it."

"To do what?" Farley put down her fork. "Tell them that they should have told us about the chimera sooner? Because they should have."

"They should, but if we want to progress any further with the case, we have two options," said Tam. "Either we go to the hospital in the next town over and talk our way into the morgue to look at the bodies..."

"No thanks," said Callum.

"Or we return to Grim Crag."

"Not a fan of that either." Farley yawned. "Though if the next town has any decent hotels, I'm game." She dropped her gaze when the inn's owner walked past, her expression as surly as ever.

"The quicker we find whoever killed those tourists, the quicker we get out of here," I whispered when she was out of sight. "I'd say it's worth another chat with the villagers up at Grim Crag."

"Do you think that Scarlet or her coven did it?" Farley asked.

"If one of them was committing murder, then I can see the others rallying around them to help hide the evidence," I said. "Though that doesn't explain *why*."

It would achieve their goal of driving off outsiders, if nothing else, but why *bite* their victims? Didn't they have wands?

"I wouldn't be surprised if it's one of them." Callum pushed his plate away. "We've got to start somewhere, so I vote we walk back to Grim Crag. You had some luck with that woman who saw the chimera, didn't you?"

"We can talk to her again, right?" I asked Tam. "Without tipping off the others, if possible."

"It's worth a shot," he agreed. "We'll leave in an hour."

"I don't suppose Maurice will be joining us?" I dropped my voice when the inspector came into the dining room. I'd hoped to ask the others for theories on how to get the surly vampire to admit to anything he might have picked up from the villagers' thoughts, but it was impossible for us to discuss anything openly while our unwanted companion was around.

"I'll speak to him." Tam nodded to the inspector and then rose to his feet before leaving the dining room.

The rest of us followed suit, and the inspector watched us leave with a glare that appeared to be mostly levelled at me. He didn't ambush me for another "chat," but I doubled my resolution to stay out of the inn for the day and returned to the dormitory to get ready for another visit to the Crag.

"So," said Farley. "What were you and Tam chatting about out there?"

A flush crept up my neck, and I busied myself with rummaging through my bag so she wouldn't see. "Not much. Mostly we wanted to discuss the mission without any unwanted eavesdroppers."

"The inspector." She continued to watch me, a smile playing on her mouth. "Lucky you and Tam were both awake."

"I'm surprised you slept through Callum's snoring." I didn't rise to the bait. "And the rain. Also, I kept thinking about how weird it is that someone's apparently biting people to death. A nonvampire, I mean."

"Don't let Maurice hear you saying that."

"He's asleep and already ticked off with me," I said. "Shame he isn't coming with us to see if the coven members are hiding any murderous secrets in their thoughts."

"I don't know. Some people are good at hiding their inmost thoughts. Scarlet strikes me as that type."

True. Look at Tam. He'd told me himself that he'd trained to keep vampires from reading his mind, though he hadn't given me the details of the circumstances under which he'd had to learn. *Yet another question that lies atop a stack that seems to be growing with every passing day.*

As for Scarlet, we'd be pushing our luck by setting foot near her coven's territory again, but we had little choice in the matter. Once we'd prepared, we left the inn as a group, leaving Maurice in the sort of dead sleep that only a vampire could accomplish. I envied him that—I wouldn't lie. My sleepless night was bound to catch up to me later, but thanks to the aggressive sea breeze, I was thoroughly wide awake as Tam led the way out of the village and into the sand dunes. The storm had washed away most of the chimera's footprints, while the tide had receded and left a stretch of wet sand dotted with sharp rocks.

"I doubt that chimera went for a swim last night," I said to the others. "I don't envy the villagers at Grim Crag either. Hope they had the sense to stay indoors."

"Hey ... there's someone over there." Farley pointed across the beach, where a ragged-looking figure wandered up and down the gravelly sand. He was yelling something, but I couldn't make out the words.

Tam veered in his direction, and we followed, drawing closer. The man seemed oblivious to our presence, though, continuing to stagger around and shout into the wind.

"Fenton!" he called out. "Fenton!"

"Excuse me," Tam called to him. "Is everything okay?"

The man spun around, looking blearily at our group. His blond hair was covered in sand, and his ragged coat looked as if he'd taken it for a swim. "Have you seen Fenton?"

"We saw him yesterday," said Tam. "Why? Is something wrong?"

"He's missing," the man mumbled. "Wait, you're not from Grim Crag, are you? You're not with the coven."

"No, we're staying in Herring Cove," said Tam. "We visited the Crag yesterday, though. You live there too?"

"Yes. I'm Charles." His face fell. "Fenton and I are fishing buddies, but he's gone missing. I don't know where he is."

"He wasn't out fishing during the storm last night, was he?" I asked suspiciously.

He blinked. "I don't know. I don't think so."

"Are the others looking for him too?" asked Callum. "The coven?"

If Scarlet and her coven had left the village, then there was a chance we might be able to talk to Alana while they weren't around. On the other hand, if Fenton was genuinely missing, then we had another dilemma on our hands. Though helping to find him might give us the chance to build up some goodwill with the villagers. One never knew.

"We'll help you look around," Tam offered. "Where did you last see him?"

The ragged man pointed at the distant cluster of houses that composed Grim Crag, but I saw no signs of Fenton or his fishing rod on the clifftop. It was lucky the houses hadn't been swamped with waves during the storm, though poor Fenton might not have been that lucky if he'd still been standing on that cliff when the rain started.

He couldn't have been, surely. Right?

We followed Charles's directions and then came to an abrupt halt when a splash of bright-red hair appeared against the grey cliffs. Scarlet approached our group, her mouth set in a scowl.

8

<hr>

S carlet's disdainful gaze passed over our group. "You again? What do you want this time?"

"We heard that Fenton is missing," Tam said to her. "We offered to help find him. He wasn't out in the storm last night, was he?"

"Storms are common enough. They don't bother us." Suspicion layered her tone. "Did the police send you?"

"No," said Tam. "We were walking in the dunes when we saw Charles on the beach, and he told us he was looking for Fenton. If you want us to contact the police in Herring Cove, though, we can see if they're willing to help with the search."

"They won't be," she said flatly. "They don't care about any of us in the slightest. Why would they lift a finger to help us?"

She might have had a point there. Though her coven hadn't paid Fenton that much attention yesterday. They'd been more focused on driving us out of town at the time, but once again, I found myself wishing Maurice had told the rest of us what he'd read in their thoughts, especially Scarlet. Fenton likely wasn't a major coven member, but letting one of their fellow villagers stand fishing on the cliffs during a storm didn't fit in with their claims that everyone at Grim Crag took care of one another.

"I assume it's all right if we help you search the beach?" I asked her. "We can cover more ground that way."

"Do as you like," she said. "As long as you don't get under our feet."

That would have to do. Given the raging storm the previous night, I had to admit I didn't hold out much hope that we'd find the missing fisherman, alive or not. Instead of mentioning it aloud, I left Scarlet and her coven members and resumed searching the beach. My feet sank into the wet sand with every step, covering ground that would soon be swallowed by the tide again.

"Did she seem sincere to you?" I asked Farley in a low voice.

"The only emotions I picked up from her were concern and wariness, so it seems so," she whispered back.

The latter, I assumed, was directed at our group. Not a surprise, but if Fenton's disappearance did turn out to be connected to the tourists' deaths, then I might have to re-evaluate whether I suspected Scarlet or one of the other villagers had been involved. They might hate outsiders, but Fenton was one of their own.

In front of us, Callum sniffed the air. "I wonder if I can pick up his scent."

"Not if the storm washed it away." *Or the sea.* There weren't many hiding places out here, except for the rocks scattered throughout the sand and the expanse of glittering ocean ahead.

"I can't imagine him going that far from his home,"

Farley commented. "Though he did want to find his missing clothes."

"Was he desperate enough to stay out all night in that ghastly storm, though?" I followed Callum towards the Crag, below which a maze of sharp rocks jutted upward out of the sand. With the tide out, it might be possible to climb up to the cliffs from the beach, but I didn't trust those slippery rocks one bit.

"You'd think his fellow villagers would have been looking out for him." Callum kicked off his shoes and climbed onto the nearest rock, using his hands and feet to navigate from one to the next. It'd be easier in wolf form, but perhaps he'd assumed shifting might freak out the villagers. In his human form, he was agile enough to move across the rocks without slipping.

Farley shook her head. "Oh no. I'm not climbing up there."

"Nor me." Shifters were generally more adept at climbing than the rest of us were, and even Tam stood back to watch him ascend the cliffs.

When Callum disappeared behind a particularly large rock, I heard him swear loudly. Then he emerged a second later, holding a very waterlogged shoe in one hand.

"That's Fenton's." With my heart lurching, I moved closer to the rocks and picked out a route to climb across, moving slowly to avoid slipping on seaweed and breaking an ankle. As I fumbled my way along, I winced when my foot slid into a gap between two rocks, then my leg. "Whoa."

"Perry, are you okay?" Tam called over to me.

"Just fine." I sank into a sitting position to free my leg and glimpsed a hand through the gap I'd nearly fallen through—a human hand attached to a person. "Oh no."

"What is it?" Callum dropped the shoe and clambered over to me.

With his help, I tugged my leg free of the rocks and pointed mutely through the gap to where Fenton's body lay on the sand below.

Callum swore under his breath. "It's him all right."

"Can you get him out of there?" From the angle, I knew the tide must have washed him up there this morning—or someone had tried to hide the body from sight.

"I'll do my best." Callum began to climb between the rocks while I retraced my path to join the others on the beach.

By the time I caught up to Farley and Tam, Callum had pulled out Fenton's body and begun to carry him over to our spot on the beach. The fisherman was unmistakeably dead, seaweed tangled in his hair and his bare arms poking out of his dressing gown. Marks on his pale skin brought the taste of bile to the back of my throat.

"Something ... chewed on him." Farley's face had gone chalk white. "Not a fish either."

"We'd better take him back to the others," Tam told us. "They'll want to know."

"I'll bring him." Callum adjusted his grip on the dead man. "I can carry him home to the village, if need be."

The gathered villagers had already spotted us by the time we reached the sand dunes. Charles let out a pained moan at the sight of Fenton's body, falling to his knees, while several of Scarlet's fellow coven members clustered around to watch as Callum carefully laid down the body on the sand.

"He's dead," said Scarlet softly. "Where did you find him?"

Tam pointed towards the cliffs. "His body was hidden

behind some rocks. Perhaps a result of the tides, perhaps not."

Tension thrummed in the air while the coven leader looked down at Fenton's body. "His death was no accident."

Charles broke into loud sobs, and I forced my gaze back to the bite marks on his arms. I hadn't seen the other bodies myself, so I couldn't make an exact comparison, but the bites were shallow, whether inflicted by a human or not. They hadn't caused his death.

"What could have done that to him?" I asked.

Scarlet's expression was flinty when she met my eyes. "Whoever it is, they will be sorry they harmed one of our own."

"When was he last seen alive?" I looked at Charles, but the guy was sobbing too hard to speak and didn't acknowledge my presence. "Did anyone see him go back into his house when the storm started?"

"You're already interrogating us?" asked the woman with the poodle from the previous day. "Despicable."

Guilt pinged at me. "I didn't mean to be insensitive. We came here to solve two murders, though, and ... and I'm pretty sure their deaths had the same cause as Fenton's did."

Charles lifted his head, his eyes swimming with tears. "I saw him yesterday evening before he turned in for the night. I thought he went indoors when the storm started. We were supposed to meet up this morning."

Then the odds were strong that the monster had ambushed Fenton before his arranged meeting with Charles. Even Fenton couldn't have been outside in that raging storm, or the monster either.

The crowd around us grew more restless as word spread of Fenton's death. Some coven members were crying, and others were talking or consoling one another. I couldn't picture any of them being responsible for the man's death, but not every villager was present. I didn't see Alana or Walter, the other man we'd spoken to the previous day. Maybe not everyone had been in a position to help with the search, but I had to wonder.

"Where's Alana?" I whispered to the others. "Anyone seen her?"

"No." Callum shook his head. "Maybe she's not up yet."

Given her nocturnal tendencies, it might be true, though the storm the previous night made it unlikely that she'd taken one of her nighttime walks either. "I hope she's not missing too."

"She's not friends with Fenton, is she?" asked Farley. "Didn't you say she's a night owl anyway? She's probably asleep."

"That's what I thought. I hope that's all it is." My attention returned to Fenton's body when Tam approached, crouching down in the sand to examine him. The other witches muttered disapprovingly among themselves, but none of them challenged him directly.

After a minute, Tam rose to his feet and returned to our group. "I can't tell the cause of death, but the bite marks are too shallow to have been more than superficial injuries."

"I thought not," I whispered back. "Did you see anything else?"

He inclined his head. "There are more marks on his neck, too, as if something grabbed him around the throat. He might have been strangled or choked, though again, that might not have caused his actual death."

"Weird." I shivered. "This can't be the sort of predator that feeds on people, then, can it?"

"I vote we get out of here," Farley said. "Tam, what do you think we should do next?"

"We need to tell the police," Tam said. "They'll want to know, regardless of whether the coven would accept their help."

"They're unlikely to offer any," I said. "Not if their attitude to those tourists' deaths is anything to go by."

"True, but Inspector Peterson won't be pleased if we neglect to inform the authorities."

"Would the coven be happy if we told *him*?" The last thing we needed was to draw their ire again—or worse, convince the inspector to come here to interrogate them in person.

"What are you whispering about?" Scarlet demanded of our group, causing her entourage's attention to fall on us again. "Do you know anything about Fenton's death that you haven't told us?"

"No," Tam said. "We do think he was killed by the same creature that attacked the two tourists who died the other night, whose deaths we're looking into on behalf of the Wardens."

Her nostrils flared. "It doesn't seem that you got very far with your investigation."

I opened my mouth and closed it again, deciding against mentioning how we'd been derailed the previous day by Lara and her odd pet. I had no doubt that if Scarlet suspected the chimera and its owner had been involved in Fenton's death, she'd unleash her own form of justice upon them both, regardless of what the actual authorities thought. In fact, the police might not even stop her from doing so.

"We're working closely with the authorities in Herring Cove," Tam told her. "We'd be more than happy to give you all the information we have available."

Her jaw twitched. "We're not surrendering Fenton's body to the police. We'll lay him to rest ourselves."

"They won't take his body away," I said. "But if we inform them of his death, it might give them an incentive to bring more people in to help with the investigation."

"I doubt it," she said. "They hardly care for their own community, let alone ours. They've always ignored our requests for help in the past."

"Has anything like this happened before?" asked Tam. "Any similar deaths?"

Scarlet's gaze briefly skimmed over our group. "No, but rest assured, Fenton's murder will be neither forgotten nor forgiven."

"That's right," added one of her fellow coven members.

Is she telling the truth? If the police had dealt with anything similar before, then the Wardens ought to have let us know, and Tam would be able to find out easily enough. I hoped.

"You speak of helping us," said the poodle lady, who apparently couldn't leave well enough alone. "But all you did yesterday was speak to Fenton and ask him impertinent questions, and now he's dead."

A murmur passed among the coven members. *Oh boy.* I should have guessed someone would fling blame at the outsiders. Never mind that the two tourists had been killed by the same monster before we'd even known their community existed.

"We spoke to Fenton because he was the person who discovered the bodies of two tourists," Tam said, echoing my thoughts. "I'm sorry for his death, but if we're to find the cause of his death and eliminate it, then we need your coven's cooperation. It's the Wardens' job to protect both the magical and the nonmagical worlds alike by dealing with threats that the regular police are unable to handle."

"A nice argument," said the poodle lady, "but I know they sent one of you people here before there was a case to investigate."

I gaped at her for a second. None of us had ever been here before, right? Then it clicked. *The inspector.*

"You've met our supervisor?" Tam's voice rose in surprise. This was news to him too. "When?"

"I saw him sniffing around the beach a few days ago," said the poodle lady. "Asked who he was and got a rude reply."

"Sounds like him," I said. "He was already in Herring Cove on an unrelated mission, but the Wardens then assigned him to assess our team. He's not helping us with this investigation."

The opposite, if anything, though I didn't want to mention his actual purpose in being here. That would involve exposing Lara and her unusual pet, which would only lead to trouble if the coven decided Cupcake was to blame for Fenton's death. If the chimera or Lara *did* turn out to be guilty, we'd end up in hot water, but she hadn't taken her pet anywhere near the village last night, and besides, Cupcake didn't have teeth.

Scarlet scowled. "Forgive me if I'm unconvinced of your sincerity."

"I don't even *like* the inspector." No point in under-playing the issue when she already knew he was here. "He's here to assess our team—Tam and the rest of us—and not to help with the actual case. He wants to make sure we're doing our jobs. Nothing more."

Scarlet turned to exchange a few words with the witch beside her then addressed us. "We intend to take Fenton's body back to our home. I'll thank you to give us some peace before you come back, with or without your inspector."

I didn't blame her for not wanting us to get in the way of the villagers' mourning someone they cared about, but I hoped one or two of their members might be open to a discussion when we paid them a visit later. Scarlet's open hostility had faded, but an aura of resentment lingered amid the other villagers, especially the poodle lady. I could see why, as we'd come here looking to solve a couple of murders, and now someone from their own village had seemingly fallen victim to the same killer, but yesterday, we'd been stymied by Scarlet's refusal to speak to us and had wasted valuable time as a result. We had to do better.

"We'll go," Tam said in a low voice. "Give them space to grieve while we inform the authorities. We can also tell Maurice, if he's awake."

I'm sure he'll be thrilled. "All right."

We left the coven members behind and began to make our way back to the sand dunes. Farley still looked faintly sick, while Callum's usual cheer was absent.

"You don't think the police are going to come rushing to help, do you?" He pulled his shoes back on as we reached the foot of the slope leading to the village. "I know, I know, it's procedure for us to let them know ... and the inspector too."

"I have a few questions I'd like to ask *him,*" I said. "He might have mentioned he ran into one of Scarlet's fellow witches on the beach a few days ago."

Really, it was no wonder they'd developed a poor opinion of the Wardens. We'd have to fix that later, because it was clear from the coven's response that the majority of the villagers were stunned by Fenton's death. The killer was more likely to have come from outside their community than not, yet Scarlet's distrust of outsiders was an impediment to finding out anything she might know about threats in the region, and I couldn't entirely rule out the possibility that one villager might have turned on the others. Given what we'd heard from Alana, we knew not everyone in the coven was directly in Scarlet's inner circle.

Was there a killer among the people of Grim Crag, or did the cause lie elsewhere? I didn't know, but after Fenton's death, it was safe to say the villagers were not immune to whatever monster had killed those two tourists. And if we didn't find the killer, then Scarlet and her coven would take matters into their own hands.

9

———

I couldn't say I was thrilled for our group to return to Herring Cove, even though I understood Tam's decision to tell the police about the most recent death before taking further action.

Unfortunately, I'd forgotten the inspector, who appeared en route to the police station and barred our paths with an irate expression on his face. "About time you showed up."

"I did tell you we were going back to Grim Crag, didn't I?" Tam said.

"That Lara woman does *not* have a valid licence for her chimera." He spoke in triumphant tones, utterly disregarding Tam's words. "I knew I'd catch her out."

"That's going to have to be put on hold," Tam told him. "Someone else is dead. A villager from Grim Crag disappeared last night, and we found his body on the beach. I believe that he was killed by the same creature that murdered those tourists."

That got his attention. The inspector's gaze sharpened. "Tell me everything at once."

Instead of leading us to the police station, though, he made for the inn instead. I quickened my pace to catch him up at the door, and when he made to enter without acknowledging me, I cleared my throat. "We were going to drop in at the police station too. It'll save on time if we tell you all at the same time, won't it?"

"If saving time is your primary motive, it's no wonder you've made no progress."

What was his problem this time? Frowning, I waited for the others to catch up before we entered the inn.

Inside, we found a sleepy-looking Maurice sitting at a table in the empty restaurant. Had the inspector woken him up, or had he found it as hard to sleep in the inn as the rest of us had? Whichever it was, it didn't surprise me that a large cup of coffee sat on the table next to his flask of blood.

I sat next to him. "I thought caffeine didn't affect vampires."

He shot me a scowl. "Nobody asked your opinion."

Vampires' tongues were as sharp as their teeth at this hour in the morning, so I shrugged off his comment.

The inspector pulled out a chair at the table next to Maurice and motioned for the rest of us to join them, and when I spotted the notebook in the inspector's hand, the penny dropped. He must have talked to Maurice and given him the same one-on-one interrogation session he'd unleashed on me the previous day. And from the way his attitude had deteriorated in the time we'd been gone, I knew whatever the vampire had said to him had put them both in a raging bad mood. Did it involve me, though? I'd guess yes, but I'd have to wait until later to find out.

I fidgeted in my seat while Tam launched into an account of our encounter with the villagers on the beach, followed by our discovery of Fenton's body and his observations surrounding the possible cause of death.

When he'd finished speaking, Inspector Peterson said, "That's an unfortunate development."

You don't say. "The police need to know, though I didn't get the impression they wanted to help with the investigation."

"Yes, they do need to know. Right away."

"You insisted on our coming back here first, remember?" Farley said irritably. The inspector's attitude was likely rubbing off on her, and while I was relieved someone other than me had pointed out the obvious, the inspector glared at me as if it were *my* fault.

What *had* Maurice told him? That I never followed the rules, maybe, but Tam had already made it clear that if one of our group failed the inspection, so would the rest of us. We were stuck in this together, after all.

"Exactly." Tam's brow pinched in a frown as he rose to his feet. "We'll tell the police. Is there anything else you want to know before we leave?"

"You think the cause of the man's death is the same as whatever killed those tourists?" asked the inspector. "If that's the case, the body will need to be examined."

"By whom?" I asked. "The villagers already took the body back with them. They wanted to mourn their dead in peace."

"They did," Tam agreed. "I'll see if the police agree with you, but I have my doubts the villagers would welcome the intrusion at a time like this."

"We'll see." When the rest of us got to our feet, the inspector beckoned to Farley. "Farley, would you stay behind and have a quick talk with me?"

Oh boy. It must be her turn to be questioned. Callum's mouth pulled down at the corners, but Tam gave the faintest shake of his head, and he reluctantly followed the rest of us out of the room. There was no arguing with the inspector, so Farley remained seated at the table while the rest of us left the inn, except Maurice.

When he made for the stairs instead of following the rest of us through the front door, I waylaid him. "Maurice, can I talk to you?"

"You already are."

Should have seen that one coming. "Outside. You don't actually want to go back to sleep up there, do you?"

The vampire scowled in response, but when Tam looked directly at him from the doorway, he relented and joined us outside. "What is it?"

"The inspector." I dropped my voice. "Who shoved a broomstick up his rear?"

"Pretty sure it was already there," said Callum. "I hope he's not harassing Farley."

"So do I," I said. "Though now he's spoken to me, Maurice, and Farley, I'm pretty sure that means it's your turn next."

"Or Tam's." He glanced at our leader, who'd begun to approach the police station. "I don't like that guy's approach in the slightest. Or his attitude."

"He was at least being civil to me yesterday," I said, "but today he's acting like I put arsenic in his tea."

"And you assume it's my fault," Maurice said.

"You're the last person who talked to him," I pointed out. "Was he like that when you woke up?"

He gave me a long look. "What do you think?"

That means yes, then. But that didn't explain *why*. "I don't want to start an argument. We're supposed to be working together, and he's assessing all of us."

"Like I can forget it," he said. "Now it turns out someone else got killed overnight, and there's an illegal chimera in town too. Is it any wonder he's ticked off?"

"Is the chimera actually illegal?" I asked. "Not that he should care either way. The deaths ought to take precedence—especially the latest one from Grim Crag."

"Your point is?"

"If you went outside last night, did you see anything weird?" I asked. "Inside or outside the village?"

"No," he said. "Not that it's any of your business, but I didn't go anywhere near that Crag last night."

"All right. Just checking." I watched Tam enter the police station ahead of us, debating whether to follow him. Callum didn't, waiting outside for Farley to return from her questioning instead, so I opted to stay put. "I don't think the police will have much to offer. They're no more help than the inspector is, except at least they aren't assessing us as well as being a nuisance."

Maurice grunted. "I don't know why you're surprised he's unhappy with us for not making any progress."

"We've made progress," said Callum. "We've ruled out one suspect, anyway. More than one, if we assume Scarlet wouldn't have killed a fellow villager as well as two tourists."

"I'd say she didn't," I said. "That, or she's a better actress than I gave her credit for. Her coven too. After all their claims about looking out for one another, murdering one of their own doesn't seem right."

"Are you sure he didn't just get himself killed in the storm?" Maurice queried.

"That's what we thought at first, but his friend seemed to

think he went missing this morning, not last night," I said. "Also, his body was covered in bite marks, and Tam said it looked like he'd been strangled too."

He grunted. "Then one of the villagers did it."

"The villagers seemed pretty shaken up," I said. "Farley said she didn't feel any emotions from them that contradicted what they said to us. If the killer is among their group, they've hidden themselves well."

"Exactly," Callum said. "Scarlet was livid. I don't see her being the killer, but I *do* see her wanting revenge on the person who did it. That's a danger we might have to look out for."

"You're probably right, but I hoped having a common goal might make her more cooperative." Though that might be too much to ask for. I glanced over at the police station, hoping the officers were being a little nicer to Tam than the inspector had been. "She also mentioned that she ran into our inspector on the beach a few days before we showed up. He didn't tell us that."

"I'm not surprised, if he's been stuck here for that long," said Maurice. "There's not much to do except walk in the rain."

"Could be worse," Callum remarked. "He could have ended up being stationed at Grim Crag instead. Not that there'd be anywhere for him to stay."

"No, there isn't," Maurice said sourly. "You couldn't pay me to go back to that miserable rock."

"Speaking of the inspector, I hope he's not grilling Farley," Callum said. "She doesn't deserve that."

"I know." I also knew better than to press Maurice for the details on his own questioning, but part of me worried that if the inspector brought up the subject of my predecessor with the others the way he had with me, it wouldn't be pleasant. Unlike me, the others had known Clarice personally, and her death had been a traumatic shock to all of them. "He mostly asked me obvious questions that he could have got from reading my file."

"Same," Maurice grunted. "He wasn't even paying attention to my answers."

"What do you mean?" asked Callum. "Was he distracted?"

"His thoughts were."

It was the first time he'd alluded to his mind-reading powers since I'd unsuccessfully tried to find out what he'd read from Scarlet and the other villagers the previous day.

"Did he have anything else lurking in his head about the murders?" I queried. "That he hasn't already told us?"

"I've had one interrogation already. I don't need another." He buried his hands in his pockets. "I haven't the faintest idea. I can't read every single thought in someone's head at once, you know."

"He's not the open-and-honest sort," said Callum. "We're not interrogating you, Maurice. We just want to get the hell out of here, and unfortunately, getting on that guy's good side is our only way out."

"It won't work," said Maurice. "He's already made up his mind."

My brows shot up. "What? He's planning for us to fail the inspection?"

"No, he has zero faith in any of us to solve the case," the vampire said bluntly.

"Then what's the point in the individual questionings?" Callum put on an uncharacteristic scowl. "What's his game?"

Maurice shrugged. "A way to pass the time between

arresting people for hiding illegal chimeras in their houses?"

"That chimera is hardly hidden away." Irked, I paced on the spot. "Did that Lara strike you as dishonest enough to pretend to have a licence when she doesn't?"

"No." The word came out grudgingly. "Not that it matters to that guy. He's a very black-and-white thinker."

"What about Scarlet?" asked Callum. "I'm not trying to pressure you, but you know, if someone in that village is the killer, we need to know sooner rather than later."

The vampire was silent for a moment. Callum was more likely to be able to get answers out of Maurice than I was, so I averted my gaze from his and watched the police station while I waited for Maurice to reply.

"I couldn't read their minds," he finally muttered. "Scarlet and the other villagers. That's the problem."

"What? None of them?" My attention snapped back towards the vampire. "That's not normal, is it?"

"Definitely not," he said. "It's like my mind-reading abilities became clouded the instant we reached Grim Crag."

"Seriously?" I stared at him. "You can still read our minds, right?"

"Yeah." He didn't meet my eyes. "Mostly. But something fogged up my mind-reading powers at Grim Crag, and it still hasn't entirely faded."

Weird. What kind of magic could block a vampire from reading minds? I'd heard of individuals learning to tune out a vampire's abilities or specialists selling rare and expensive charms to make one's mind impervious to being read but not an entire village being immune.

"Maybe Scarlet and her coven put some kind of magical defences around the village," I suggested. "A vampire-proof ward, if there's such a thing."

"Maybe." Callum's brow crinkled. "Ah—there's Farley."

The inn's door closed, and Farley approached with her head bowed. My heart sank a little. Had the inspector made cruel comments designed to get under her skin the way he'd done with me? I should have warned her, but I hadn't wanted to create tension with the others by bringing up the subject of my predecessor's untimely death.

When she reached our group, Farley lifted her head and gave a strained smile. "Hey."

"Are you okay?" Callum asked.

"Yeah, I'm fine." She nodded to the police station. "Is Tam in there?"

"Yeah, he is," I said. "We were waiting for you. Is the inspector still at the inn?"

"Not for long." She pulled a face. "He's on a mission to get that Lara arrested and her chimera taken away from her."

"Isn't he more concerned with the murders?" I asked. "I know he'd rather interrogate us than let us take action, but this is ridiculous."

"It is," Callum said. "I wouldn't mind him staying out of our hair, but arresting an innocent person goes against everything the Wardens are supposed to stand for."

"You don't have to tell *us* that," said Farley. "The question is 'What're we supposed to do?'"

"Solve the murders as planned." Whatever the situation with Lara and her chimera, the case had to take precedence, if just for the sake of any potential future victims. "Starting with whatever's going on up at Grim Crag. Maurice said he can't read anyone's minds in the entire village, so we need to figure out why."

"Thanks a lot," Maurice grumbled.

"You told us voluntarily," Callum pointed out. "The rest

of the team needs to know too. That way, we're more likely to be able to find the cause."

"Weird," said Farley. "A spell, maybe? Perry, can you use one of your revealing charms?"

"I can, but I'd need to be right next to the village, and Scarlet wouldn't like that." I looked over at the police station's door when Tam walked out. "We'll discuss it as a team."

Tam spotted Farley first. "Farley, are you okay?"

"Yes, I'm fine," she said, her tone more curt than usual. "Please, all of you, stop treating me like I'm made of glass. What did the police officers have to say?"

"The officers said they *might* go to Grim Crag later, but I won't hold my breath," Tam said. "It might be for the best that they don't, really."

"True," I said, "but we found out something else. Namely, Grim Crag appears to be vampire-proofed."

Maurice glowered at me, but when Tam swivelled to face him, he smoothed out his expression. "I can't read anyone's minds there. Not a single villager."

"Maybe every one of them is wearing a charm that blocks mind reading," Farley said. "They exist."

"Aren't they rare and expensive?" asked Callum. "I don't see the entire population of a tiny self-sufficient fishing village forking out for a mountain of custom-made charms."

"Scarlet could have designed them herself," I suggested. "Whatever the cause, removing the spell might expose the killer."

"Yeah, if the coven doesn't flay you alive for it," Maurice said. "You won't be able to get away with messing with that Scarlet's spells. I guarantee it."

"She's distracted at the moment," I said, "but I freely

admit that we might have to destroy any goodwill we've built up between us."

"Not much to destroy," said Farley. "I don't think she's the killer, but someone is, and the odds that they're hiding among the villagers are pretty high. Why else would they want to hide their thoughts from being read? I don't see any other vampires in the area."

"There's a chance it might be a side effect of a different spell," said Tam. "The police said we can go back to the village, but they said that it's not their problem if we get into trouble with the coven."

"And the inspector?" I turned to Farley.

She shrugged. "He didn't say we couldn't."

Inspector Peterson hadn't spoken to Callum alone yet—or Tam. The last thing we needed was to give him any more opportunities to detain us, so we headed for the sandy path leading outside the village without dropping back at the inn.

As we walked, I fell into step with Farley. "Was the inspector as unpleasant to you as he was to me?"

"Depends what you mean by unpleasant." She dug her hands into her pockets as the ocean breeze swept over us. "He told me off for not carrying a wand."

I frowned. "What does that matter to him?"

"Sets a bad impression, apparently." She pulled a face. "I told him that I'm more likely to accidentally hit a teammate with a defensive spell than an enemy, but he took no notice of me."

"Guess it's better than calling you a disappointment."

"He said that?"

"More or less." I shook my head. "Maurice seems to think he's out to fail us."

The vampire shot me a glower over his shoulder. "If you have something to say about me, say it to my face."

"I'm talking about the inspector, not you," I said. "What does he have to gain from us failing the inspection? Doesn't that mean more paperwork for him?"

"Yes," said Tam, "and regardless of his intentions, you were right when you said solving the murders is our best route forward. Let's move."

We lapsed into silence as we followed the path through the sand dunes. The beach was deserted, as I'd expected, the villagers having returned to Grim Crag to mourn their dead.

And here we were, about to sneak into their home and possibly remove their defences. Scarlet would be thrilled with me.

Tam brought us to a halt when the collection of stone houses came within sight. "Perry, can you use the spell here?"

"I think so." I reached for my wand. "If there's a protective boundary around the village, I ought to be able to sense it from here. Is anyone around?"

"No." Farley stood on tiptoe, peering down the path between the houses. "We're clear."

"Good." I waved my wand and cast a revealing spell.

Light spread out from my wand, only to fizzle out as if extinguished by the dampness in the air. Undeterred, I cast a second spell, and when that failed, I took a few steps to the left and tried again.

I followed a path around the outskirts of the village, but my spells continued to reveal nothing—no defences, no charms ... and no clues as to why Maurice had lost his mind-reading power whenever he crossed the boundary of the village.

When I returned to the others, I tucked my wand out of sight. "Sorry. I can't sense any wards or boundaries. There's nothing there."

"A likely story." The vampire's eyes simmered with anger. "I don't trust *any* of them."

"We might find more clues if we go into the village itself." Tam faced the houses, his expression as grim as the Crag. "Let's hope Scarlet is in an accommodating mood."

10

———

Nobody from Grim Crag appeared to have noticed my attempts to sniff out security spells, but when we advanced down the street, a clamour drifted down the row of houses. The house at the far end was around twice the size of the others, wide and squat with red-painted doors. On the doors, someone had affixed a hand-written sign that read Coven Meeting in Progress.

Based on the volume of the noise, I thought most of the town was inside the house, which meant we'd be outnumbered the instant we went inside. It would also prove an issue if the police did show up, wanting to examine Fenton's body—or worse, the inspector.

"Should we talk to Alana first?" I whispered to Tam. "If she's not with the coven, I think this might be our only chance to talk to her before they realise we're here."

"Talk to her about what?" Maurice's manner had only worsened after I'd failed to unearth any magical barriers at the village's border, though I had to wonder if he'd be able to read Alana's mind when she wasn't around the others. If the spell keeping him from reading people's thoughts didn't cover the entire village, it must have limits, surely.

"For a start, we can explain to her that the chimera wasn't responsible for the murders," I said. "Ask if she went out last night too. I doubt she did, but she might have heard something..."

Someone else came walking from the direction of the seafront—specifically, the Viking-looking man who we'd spoken to the previous day. *What was his name again? Walter?*

"You're back," he observed.

"We are," Tam said. "I take it you found out about Fenton's death?"

"Everyone did." His expression pinched, his gaze travelling from the red-painted doors to our group. "You were going to go inside, but you changed your minds. Why?"

"What's it to you?" Maurice challenged him.

Tam stepped in. "We intended to see if any of the town's citizens were willing to talk to us alone before we approached the coven again. I understand that this is a difficult time for all of you, but we believe Fenton's death is connected to the two tourists whose murders we're investigating."

Come to think of it, Walter had led us to talk to Alana in the first place, so maybe he was worth speaking to again. He gave us a considering look. "You're the ones who found Fenton's body, are you not?"

"We are," Tam said. "Did you know him well?"

"No." He lowered his gaze. "I was afraid this might happen. We're vulnerable here, after all."

Strange of him to say, given that Scarlet evidently thought her people were capable of taking care of themselves. "I thought the coven was dedicated to protecting all the villagers."

He turned towards me but didn't quite meet my eyes. "There are some ... some threats that even the coven cannot handle, as much as Scarlet wishes it were otherwise."

"What do you mean?" Tam asked. "Do you know what might have killed Fenton?"

He shook his head. "I don't, but I sincerely hope Scarlet urges everyone to stay at home until the threat has passed."

"Why aren't *you* with her?" Maurice cut in.

Walter regarded him coolly. "I had some business to take care of. Whereabouts are you all going, precisely? There aren't many citizens likely to be outside the coven's headquarters at the present time."

It couldn't be plainer that he expected us to let him in on our plan, but would Alana be open with us when the guy who'd led us to question her was lurking around? I doubted it.

When nobody replied, Walter asked, "It's Alana, isn't it? Did she give you any hints yesterday that might have led you to find out who killed Fenton?" An odd intensity underlaid his tone, though maybe not so odd, given the circumstances.

"No," said Tam. "She gave us one possible lead, but it turned out to be a mistake."

"Explain."

Walter's commanding tone made me bristle, and even Tam arched a brow at him. "We take orders from the Wardens, Walter, not from members of the public."

Yeah, exactly. Walter might be pushing for answers for the sake of warning his fellow villagers, but we didn't need to tell him about Lara and her possibly illegal pet. That had nothing to do with the issue at hand, and the last thing we needed was to complicate the situation even further.

If more proof connecting Cupcake the chimera with Fenton's death surfaced, then it'd be a different story, but until then, we didn't need to send a bunch of angry and grieving villagers after an innocent person.

Walter's mouth thinned. "I didn't mean to pry. I would dearly like to help to protect my fellow villagers. Nothing more."

"I understand," said Tam. "Alana mentioned seeing someone out on the beach at night when she was on one of her walks, but there turned out to be no connection between them and the murders. We spoke to the police of Herring Cove and confirmed it."

Walter didn't look particularly satisfied with that explanation, but technically we'd given him all the information he'd asked for, even if we'd omitted some pertinent details.

"Very well," he said. "I hope you have a productive conversation with Alana. I can't say I know if she went out again last night, but I do wonder if she might have more to share with you that she hasn't already."

Sidestepping our group, he made for the door to the coven's headquarters. After checking he wasn't following us, we walked down the path towards Alana's home.

"What a busybody," Maurice muttered. "I don't trust that guy."

"Do you trust anyone?" If Maurice couldn't read *anyone's* mind, then any of Grim Crag's citizens might be guilty of murder, and we couldn't trust anyone at all, including Alana.

Tam led us to Alana's house and knocked on the door. Again, Alana made us wait for several minutes before she answered, and like yesterday, she wore a long, hooded cloak from head to toe. "You're back."

"We are," Tam said. "May we come in?"

"Is this about Fenton?" she asked. "I heard he died, so you don't need to tell me that."

Hmm. Maybe Walter was right to be suspicious of her. Why wasn't she with the rest of the coven?

"It's not that," I said. "Not entirely, anyway. We wanted to discuss the tip-off you gave us yesterday."

"Oh." She backed into the doorway. "Sure, come on in."

Tam turned to the others. "Who wants to volunteer to keep watch outside?"

"Maurice already is." Callum indicated the street's end, where Maurice stood watching the path to the seafront as if he didn't trust Walter not to reappear. "I'll join him."

Farley accompanied Tam and me into the house, which retained the strong smell of herbs. She eyed Alana with suspicion, but unlike Maurice's abilities, her empath talents didn't appear to be affected by whatever spell the people of Grim Crag had used. That meant she'd be able to pick up on Alana's feelings and let us know if she was being sincere.

"We tracked down the owner of the beast you saw on the beach," Tam said without preamble. "It turned out to be a chimera."

Her eyes widened. "A chimera?"

"Yes, but it was someone's pet," I clarified. "We also found out it doesn't have teeth, so it can't be responsible for biting anyone to death."

"Oh." Her shoulders slumped. "I'm glad, I think, but ... is keeping one of those things as a pet actually legal?"

"That's a matter for the Wardens to deal with," Tam said. "Our supervisors, that is. We're simply here to investigate the tourists' deaths, and with Fenton dead, too, it's even more important that we verify any information we're given. Did you go outside last night?"

She hesitated for a second. "No ... not during the storm. I don't understand why Fenton did, frankly, but nothing he did made much sense."

"You think he did go out last night?" I asked. "Not early this morning? That's what his friend Charles said."

"I don't know," she said. "I was asleep this morning, and it rained most of the night. Usually nobody is around when I go out, so I guess Charles might be right about the attack taking place this morning."

I risked a glance at Farley, who wore a frown but didn't indicate any doubt in the sincerity of Alana's response. She didn't seem particularly fazed by Fenton's death, but it didn't sound as if she was close to the other villagers either.

"Do you have anything else you can tell us?" asked Tam. "Concerning Fenton or otherwise?"

"No," she replied. "I haven't seen or spoken to anyone since your visit yesterday. You'll have to talk to the coven if you want to learn more, I think."

That was most likely true, and while I debated mentioning Walter's suspicions, it would only remove the one potential ally we'd found among the villagers.

"Thank you for your time." Tam made for the door.

Farley and I followed him. A sudden rustle of movement behind me made me freeze midstep, but it was only Alana, snatching up something from the floor in front of me.

"Sorry." She pocketed the item I'd nearly trodden on—a glass vial—and raised her hands in a placating manner. "I was brewing potions last night. Must've dropped one."

I turned back to the door and startled to see Maurice, who'd appeared in the doorway in the blink of an eye.

"Whoa." I blinked, seeing that he'd caught Alana's door in his hand, holding it open. The act of politeness was so out of character for the vampire that I started. "Erm... Maurice?"

He gave me a scathing look without letting go of the door. "Did any of you know?"

"Know what?"

"She's a vampire, fool."

I spun back to Alana—who held the vial in her hand, the light illuminating the crimson liquid within. Her hood fell back, her face paling beneath as she moved forward. "I can explain."

If anyone would recognise a vampire by sight, it was Maurice, but now I looked more closely at her, it was obvious. The smell of herbs in her house and the way she moved carefully around as if to hide her enhanced speed had fooled us all, even Tam. He'd gone still, as if anticipating an oncoming attack, while Farley and Callum both gawped at her through the open door.

Before anyone could speak, footsteps echoed on the street outside, and Walter reappeared at speed. *Was he eavesdropping the entire time?*

"Is there a problem?" he asked our group.

I said nothing, hoping he'd take the hint and mind his own business this time, but Maurice had no such compunctions. He strode out of Alana's house and addressed Walter. "Did you know she was a vampire?"

Walter's eyes widened. "Alana? No. No, I certainly did not."

"Surprise," Maurice said darkly. "Guess she's been fooling you all. Personally, I'd have guessed as soon as she started avoiding everyone during the day and sneaking out at night."

"You're a vampire yourself." Walter took a shaky step towards our group, his gaze landing on Alana's open door. "Alana, I'd appreciate it if you explained yourself. Were you not a witch until recently?"

Alana blanched. "I was attacked two months or so ago while I was out on a trip. A group of vampires set upon me, and I was bitten during my escape. I... I knew what it meant, but I hoped I might be able to stop the transformation. I've brewed potions that have dulled some of the effects, but in the end…"

"You feed on blood now?" Walter asked with an expression of distaste.

She lifted her chin. "I've never bitten any of the people of Grim Crag."

"Do you expect me to believe that after Fenton's death?" His voice trembled with anger. "There were bite marks on his body. He was murdered."

"No," she said. "Absolutely not. I might be a vampire, but I'd never kill someone."

Walter didn't look convinced. "I'm afraid I'll have to tell Scarlet. You can't keep a secret like that from the coven leader."

"Hang on," she said, but he was already turning away towards the coven's headquarters.

I hurried after him, not knowing what else to do, but Tam caught my arm. "This is between them."

"I don't think a vampire killed Fenton." I spoke in a low voice, my gaze travelling between Alana and Maurice. "Trust me. I know what a vampire's bite looks like."

"She's a vampire masquerading as a human, though," Maurice said. "Was she filing down her teeth?"

"No clue." I hadn't thought to look, but since she hadn't given me the usual vampire vibes, it wasn't surprising. "The victims weren't drained of blood. This doesn't fit."

Walter pushed open the door, entering the coven's headquarters. This time Tam didn't stop me from following, instead accompanying me through the doorway. As we watched, Walter made his way through the throng of coven members to their leader, who stood beside a table on which Fenton's body lay, covered with a long sheet.

Upon spotting our group, Scarlet strode over to us, beckoning to Walter to follow her.

"What's this?" she demanded. "Walter here tells me you exposed a citizen of our village as a vampire."

"We didn't expose anything," I said. "Not intentionally, anyway, and this has nothing to do with the murders we're here to solve—"

"I'm afraid it does," Walter said. "Fenton was bitten during the attack that ended his life, and given how vampires attack their prey, I can only assume Alana is guilty of his murder."

Anger suffused Scarlet's features, but it was directed at us, not Walter. "This is coven business, and Alana's crimes will be punished by me alone. You are not welcome here."

"We didn't even know she was a vampire," I protested. "Besides, I know what a vampire's bite looks like, and that's not what I saw on Fenton's body. She didn't commit any crimes."

"She kept her true nature a secret from her coven," said Walter. "That's against the core rules of the village, even if you don't take the recent deaths into consideration. Isn't that right, Scarlet?"

"It is." Scarlet's lips compressed. "How unfortunate. Alana hasn't been active in the coven in recent weeks, but I gave her the privacy afforded to all our citizens and overlooked her behaviour. It seems I was mistaken."

She backed through the partly open doors, snapping her fingers to call several other witches to her side. Fanning out of the building, they whispered among themselves, passing on the news of Alana's secret.

"Is it true?" The poodle lady followed them, gesturing at our group. "Did *these* people accuse one of our own of committing a crime?"

"Alana admitted it herself," said Walter, who I kind of wanted to punch in the face at this point. "One of the newcomers recognised her as a vampire."

Murmurs passed among the others, and Scarlet snapped her fingers for a second time to silence them. "We'll speak to Alana and verify these newcomers' claims ourselves."

The coven members swarmed past our group and converged on Alana's house. She'd closed the door, which I didn't blame her for, but Scarlet pushed it open without knocking and glared down at Alana. The vampire stood in the doorway with her hands clenched at her sides and an expression of defiance on her face.

"Is it true that you're a vampire?" Scarlet asked her.

Alana flinched. "Yes... I'm a vampire. I kept it from you because I didn't want to surrender my position in the coven, but I've never hurt anyone from the village. It's the truth."

"You lied to us," said Scarlet. "For weeks, if Walter is right."

"I was turned against my will," Alana whispered. "I tried everything I could to reverse the transformation and minimise the effects. And I've never fed on anyone in the village. *Never.*"

"Were you outside last night? When Fenton died?"

"No." She shrank back into the house when Scarlet pulled out her wand. "No, I swear I didn't kill him."

"There were teeth marks on his body," said Walter. "That sounds conclusive enough, doesn't it?"

"They didn't belong to a vampire," I said loudly. "Trust me. I've staked several dozen vampires myself, and I've had up-close-and-personal experience with their teeth."

I'd even been bitten a couple of times, though the transformation into a vampire could only be completed if the victim then drank some of the vampire's blood too. Whether

Alana had done so voluntarily or not, though, she was innocent of murder. Even if she *had* filed her teeth down, why bite Fenton if not to feed on him?

Nobody paid my protests any attention as the coven members continued to argue back and forth. My heart leapt in my chest when I glimpsed the blurred movement of a vampire attempting to flee—but Scarlet's wand went off with a bang and a flash of red light, and Alana collapsed into a heap on the ground.

"Secure her at once, and bring her to our base," she ordered. "Now."

"Hang on a moment." I knew it wasn't wise to challenge her at a time like this, but all my instincts urged me to stop her before she made a terrible mistake. "What do you plan to do with her exactly?"

"She'll have a trial in front of the coven, like anyone else who commits a crime against our tenets," she said. "As leader of this community, I can dispense the law as I wish."

The other witches and wizards moved in to pick up Alana's limp body, while Tam waylaid Scarlet and addressed her in a low voice. "I understand you have your own way of doing things here, but we're investigating two murders, and we pledged to help you find Fenton's killer."

"And you did, but if you're expecting me to grant you a favour in exchange, you're mistaken."

"I don't believe Alana is the person who killed Fenton," Tam said clearly. "That said, it's the police who are supposed to be responsible for the punishment for whoever was responsible for the other two murders. We have to inform them of this."

"Then by all means, go ahead, but I won't allow you or the police of Herring Cove to usurp our authority here."

Without another word, she swept away after her fellow

coven members, who disappeared through the red-painted doors of the coven's headquarters. The message couldn't be clearer. If we stayed, we ran the risk of ending up locked up alongside Alana or worse, but the alternative was to turn our backs and leave her to her fate.

As for the police, they wouldn't be in a hurry to get her off the hook, even if she was innocent, and neither was Inspector Peterson. That left it to us, and Maurice didn't look bothered by her predicament. Farley and Callum both wore conflicted expressions, while Tam's attention was on Walter, who hadn't followed the others into the coven's headquarters.

As Walter made to leave, I stepped into his path. "You're all making a mistake. Alana isn't the killer, and it doesn't look to me as if Scarlet is going to give her a fair trial."

"She's fair," said Walter. "There's no need to look at me like that. Alana put us all in danger by concealing her vampire status."

"It's not against the law to keep secrets," I said. "What's the punishment likely to be?"

"That is for Scarlet to decide," he said. "We've never had a murder in our community before, nor anything like this."

"And you think you have the right to inflict your version of justice on her, do you?" I made to follow him when he turned away. "The real killer is still out there. You can't hide from that."

Tam caught my arm when I marched after him down the street. "Perry. Calm down."

"You can't seriously be thinking of leaving them to punish someone for no reason," I hissed. "I'm pretty sure letting members of the public take the law into their own hands is against the rules of the Wardens."

"The rules are murky in cases like this," he said. "I'll

check with the inspector and the police, but while they might be able to step in, the fallout with the coven isn't likely to end in our favour."

"Alana isn't the murderer," I said. "Tell me you believe that, at least."

"I do," he said, "and now it's even more important that we find the real killer as quickly as possible."

11

As we approached Herring Cove yet again, I dragged my heels, even more reluctant to set foot in the village than I'd been beforehand. Explaining the news about Alana's unexpected arrest to the inspector would give him yet another excuse to berate us, and I didn't hold out much hope for convincing him *or* the police to help us. Especially the latter, but what could the pair of them do against an entire coven who were fixated on punishing the wrong person for a murder she didn't commit?

While we walked, I considered and discarded a half dozen possible ways to help Alana get away without punishment, all of which would make us even less popular with the locals than we already were. Finding the real killer ought to be our priority, and we didn't need to give Scarlet and her coven even more reason to drive us off.

What a mess. The worst part was that Fenton's death had been all but forgotten in the wake of Alana's secret being exposed. I might have blamed Maurice for telling Walter she was a vampire, but really, it was more Walter's fault for refusing to leave her alone. That he and the others wouldn't accept the possibility of anyone else being responsible for Fenton's death grated on my nerves as persistently as the sand in my shoes.

To finish out an already dismal outing, we found the inspector outside the police station in Herring Cove as if he'd expected our return. "Back already?"

"Unfortunately, we hit a snag," said Tam. "Scarlet and her coven have taken the law into their own hands, but they've arrested and imprisoned the wrong person for Fenton's murder."

"Have they now?" His brows rose. "How do you know the person they've accused isn't guilty?"

"We don't know for certain, but they've refused to accept any alternative suggestions," Tam said. "Is there anything the Wardens can do in this situation?"

"No," he said. "It's our role to protect the public from magical dangers. If they take matters into their own hands ... well, it's up to the local police if they want to raise an objection and go to speak to the coven in person."

"Are they likely to?" I doubted they'd want to exert the effort, and in a clash between the officers and the coven, Scarlet was likely to win without even lifting her wand.

"Ask them yourself." He indicated the police office.

Tam moved towards the door, but I kept my attention on the inspector. "If she turns out to be innocent of murder, they still intend to have her arrested for being a vampire and keeping it a secret from her coven. That's not a crime, is it?"

"Not according to the law, no," he said, "but the coven rules absolute over the people of Grim Crag, and in that case, the punishment is theirs to decide. Am I right in guessing that it was her vampire status that prompted the coven to consider her guilty of their fellow villager's death?"

"Yes, but Scarlet's reaction was way out of order," I said. "I know she's their coven leader, but I'm pretty sure the Wardens are supposed to step in when covens take the law into their own hands. Aren't they?"

"Yes, you'd know about taking the law into your own hands, Peregrine," he said softly. "Are you sure you should be casting judgement on the coven for doing the same?"

"I've never single-handedly arrested someone for disobeying a rule I made up myself." Humiliation burned my neck, and my hands curled into fists. "Everything I've done has been in keeping with my role as a Warden."

Tam stepped in before my mouth got me into even more trouble. "We'll talk to the police first, but if they refuse to come with us to speak to the coven, then it falls to the Wardens."

"The police are currently occupied with the case of the illegal chimera," said the inspector. "As am I."

Ack. "They're hassling Lara again?"

"They're currently paying her a visit, yes."

"Then why are you lurking outside their office?" I probably shouldn't have used the word *lurking*, accurate or not, but what *was* he doing? He couldn't have known we'd come back at that precise moment. Had he been sneaking around the police's office when they weren't around —and why?

"They left shortly before your return." His mouth tightened. "If Lara is unable to prove that she has the paperwork we require, then we must act."

"By doing what? Arresting her?" I couldn't believe he'd prioritise a toothless chimera over finding a killer, but arguing with him was like trying to have a productive conversation with a fence post.

"If necessary," he said. "The police want to question her

about her pet's possible connection to the recent deaths too."

They'd better not. If he was right, that made it two people who'd been accused of murder, neither of whom was the actual culprit. Was it possible for us to help them both at once, with the authorities set against us?

Tam narrowed his eyes at the inspector. "We'll speak to them, then."

As the rest of us moved to follow him, Inspector Peterson beckoned to Callum. "I'd like a word, please, Callum. It won't be for long."

He has got to be joking. I couldn't believe the inspector was still set on wasting our time by interrogating all our team members.

"I'll wait for him," Farley offered. "You go and help Lara."

"If you're sure." Tam led us down the street and halted at a junction. "I think she lives this way…"

We followed him down a side street, where he stopped to read the road sign. "We're close. I hope she *does* have the paperwork."

"That doesn't matter, if the police have already decided the chimera is guilty of killing three people." Which wasn't possible because her pet had no *teeth*. Irritation burned beneath my skin. "This is absurd. Is anyone actually interested in finding the real culprit?"

"We are." Tam turned into a short avenue that ended at the foot of a sand dune. "This is a setback. I won't lie. But we still have time to solve this."

Lara's house was small but cosy-looking, its garden overgrown with weeds. The front gate was ajar, and the murmur of voices came from behind the door.

When Tam knocked, the older police officer answered.

"You again? Didn't that inspector tell you we were in the middle of an important questioning?"

"Yes, but we've come to inform you that Scarlet and her coven have arrested an innocent person in an attempt to take the law into their own hands," he said. "I assumed you'd want to know."

"You were mistaken. We're talking to this young lady." Phil Sr gestured through an open door off the hallway, where Lara stood talking to the younger officer.

"I swear I have a licence." Her pleading gaze met mine. "I've been tearing the place apart trying to find it, but it's gone."

"Doesn't the Warden's office have a record?" Tam asked. "It should, if you officially registered."

Lara gestured towards Phil Sr. "He claims he can't reach them."

"Can't you?" Tam raised a brow. "I can call the office myself, if you'd prefer."

"I thought you had more important matters to deal with," said the officer.

"Yes, we do," I said. "Namely, preventing the wrong person from being arrested."

"Arrested?" Lara exclaimed. "I thought the punishment for not having a chimera licence was a fine."

"Looked into it, have you?" Phil Sr asked nastily. "In case you got caught out?"

"I *have* a licence." She lowered her gaze. "They'll take Cupcake away from me as well, and I can't let that happen. He's scared of strangers."

I felt an unexpected rush of pity for her. It was easier to believe she was innocent than Alana, though they both had unfortunate timing in the secrets they'd decided to keep. "The inspector seemed to think your questioning included the subject of the recent tourists' deaths, but I have a hard time believing a beast without teeth could have bitten people to death."

Phil Sr flushed. "Those tourists weren't bitten to death, which you know as well as I do."

"I didn't know you cared." My mouth was running away with me again as my annoyance spilled over. "We can check with the Wardens' office on the licence issue, but you need more proof than that to accuse someone of murdering three people."

Lara's eyes widened. "Hang on. Did someone else die?"

"Yes." I addressed the officers. "Which *you* know as well as I do. The coven's decided to pin the blame on another citizen, and they're intending to put her on trial for murder."

"What do you expect us to do?" Phil Jr marched out of the living room, leaving Lara behind him. "Walk to the Crag ourselves? It might have escaped your attention, but we're busy."

"Inspector Peterson informs us that we don't have the authority to interfere, but you certainly do," I said. "Also, they still have Fenton's body. That seems more important than a misplaced pet licence."

"Misplaced?" Phil Sr scowled. "She lied about ever having it."

"I didn't lie," said Lara. "I've had Cupcake for years. The Wardens have a record. I know it, but the officers won't check."

"Then I'll ask the inspector," said Tam. "Until you hear from the Wardens' office, I suggest you make the people of Grim Crag a priority."

"We don't take suggestions from you," said Phil Jr. "Despite what your supervisor might think."

Did the inspector argue with them too? I'd assumed that

they were on the same page on the chimera-licence issue at the very least, but Inspector Peterson wasn't doing a good job of making friends here.

"We caught him hanging around your office just now," I told them. "You didn't leave the door unlocked, did you?"

The officers exchanged glances. Then Phil Sr beckoned to his companion. "We'll come back later."

"That's right," Phil Jr told Lara. "You aren't off the hook yet."

I stepped aside, as did Tam, while the officers left the house. Lara emerged into the hallway to watch them leave, her expression bewildered. "Er, thanks, I think."

"We don't want anyone else to get arrested except for the actual killer," Tam said to her. "As for your pet ... have you spoken to Inspector Peterson today?"

"No." Her brow wrinkled. "Is he really hanging around outside the police station? Weird."

"He claimed to be waiting for us," I said. "Really, he *and* the police have their priorities in the wrong order."

"And those villagers, if it's true," she said. "They actually arrested someone from their own community?"

"For the crime of hiding the fact that she was a vampire." I gave an eye-roll. "Which doesn't implicate her in the murders either, since the bite marks on the bodies belonged to a regular human."

"They did?" Her eyes rounded. "A *person* bit them to death?"

"No, they weren't killed by the bite wounds," I clarified. "It's not exactly clear what *did* kill them, but nobody seems interested in separating truth from lie."

"I can relate." She eyed Tam and me, her mouth turning down at the corners. "I was telling the truth, you know. I do have a licence for Cupcake. If someone checks the records with the Wardens, they'll find it for themselves. In fact, I thought the inspector already did."

"Then what's his issue?" Really, you'd think he'd be so desperate to get out of this miserable village that he'd be happy to wash his hands of the matter and help us with the murder investigation instead.

"No clue," she said. "Where is he now?"

"Questioning Callum," I said. "If you ask me, we should go and rescue him."

Tam inclined his head. "If you want to come with us when I call the office, you're welcome to."

"Thanks." Lara looked somewhat surprised at his offer, though it had taken me off guard too. Maybe calling the office was the quickest way to get the police and the inspector's attention back to the pertinent issue, but it irked me that we had to waste our time trying to find proof of Lara's licence to hold a pet chimera.

Of all of us, Tam might be the only team member who stood a chance of gaining the inspector's cooperation. The guy had a personal grudge against me, I was sure, and his earlier comments had stung more than I wanted to admit. I wasn't the only team member who'd skirted the rules in the past, but he'd singled me out anyway. And Maurice, perhaps, but the vampire was nowhere to be seen. I hoped he'd gone back to wait for Callum and not wandered off alone again.

When we neared the police station, Tam disappeared inside the inn. While part of me was curious to hear what he said to the inspector, I didn't need to give him another opportunity to belittle me. Besides, poor Callum was still trapped in an interrogation, while Farley waited outside alongside Maurice. Good, at least the vampire had stayed in the village.

Outside the police station, Phil Jr eyed Lara. "No sneaking off, you hear me?"

"She's allowed to walk around the village of her own free will," I told him. "Besides, we intend to talk to the inspector and ask him to call the Wardens' office to hunt down that licence of yours. In the meantime, you're free to go back to focusing on the murders."

"Exactly." Lara, to my disconcertment, marched straight past Phil Jr and through the open door to the police office. "If you want to keep an eye on me, then I'll stay right here while you wait to hear from the inspector."

The officers spluttered in protest, but they could hardly kick her out of their office when she was technically a suspect. It was strange that she'd helped us, though we might have spared her from losing her beloved pet, but Maurice's expression remained sceptical as Farley half dragged him over to join me near the police station.

"Callum will have to catch up with us later," she murmured to me. "I'm not missing this."

"Missing what?" Maurice tugged his arm free of her with an aggrieved expression on his face. "We still don't have any *actual* clues to point to the killer."

"We need to stop the coven from punishing Alana." I walked into the police office to join Lara and addressed the two officers. "One of you can go to Grim Crag to speak to the coven, can't you?"

"Out of the question," said Phil Sr. "What proof do you have that the villager the coven arrested is innocent?"

"The only crime she committed was hiding the fact that she's a vampire." I didn't particularly want to get into another debate on the subject, but hiding that information would only cause more trouble later on. "No, she didn't bite the victims. The bite marks didn't belong to a vampire."

"And you know because…?" Phil Jr began.

"Vampires generally only bite to feed," Maurice interjected, to my surprise. "The victims weren't drained of blood. Also, our teeth look like this."

He bared his fangs, and the officers backed away slowly. I never thought I'd have been glad to see a vampire in threatening mode, but I had to fight back a grin of my own at the officers' expressions.

"See?" I said into the stunned silence that followed. "We might not know the actual cause of death, but it's rare for a vampire to bite and not draw blood."

"The initial report said they drowned," said Phil Sr. "The bodies are out of our hands now, and we have yet to hear news on whether an autopsy has been conducted on either of them."

Yet another question to ask the inspector, though we should never have left it up to him to visit the hospital to begin with.

"And the third victim?" I asked. "His body is currently in the hands of the coven. That's why we need one of you to come with us to talk to them."

The two Phils looked as if I'd asked them to clean out the chimera's litterbox.

"The body belongs to the coven," said Phil Sr. "If Scarlet does not hand it over willingly, we cannot force her to."

That figured. If I was able to get close to Fenton's body, I might have tried to use a spell to detect his cause of death, but I'd already missed my chance. Besides, that kind of spell wasn't my strong point, and the detection charms I'd used outside the village itself had turned up zero results.

"You want us to protect you from this coven?" Phil Jr smirked. "I thought you could handle yourselves."

"You couldn't protect yourself from a paper cut," I

snapped. "I'm trying to obey the laws here, even the ridiculous ones that state the Wardens can't get involved in local coven affairs."

"*Do* they now?" said Phil Sr. "Then why are you still here?"

"We might not be allowed to stop the coven from detaining people for absurd reasons, but that doesn't mean we're leaving." My hands itched to grab them by the collars and bang their heads together. "We're here to solve the murders."

The sound of the door closing drew my attention to Farley, who'd backed outside, no doubt to avoid getting caught in our argument. Maurice had gone, too, while Lara stood uncomfortably at my side, better at controlling her temper than I was.

"Is that so?" said Phil Jr. "Then my answer is no, I will not accompany you to that ghastly cliff. Mind your manners the next time you ask us for a favour."

"We aren't asking you for a favour." The voice that spoke was Tam's. He stood in the doorway with his arms folded across his chest. "We're asking you to do your jobs so we can do ours. Inspector Peterson would like a word with both of you."

"We won't..."

Tam stepped aside, and the inspector entered the office, looking rather flushed.

I hastened to step outside before I got trapped in the office with them, but the inspector's flustered demeanour took me off guard. What in the world had Tam said to him?

Outside, Tam was already walking back to the inn, with Farley and Maurice behind him.

"Why didn't you get your teeth out in Grim Crag when Scarlet was arresting Alana?" I asked the vampire.

"Because I don't have a death wish."

"You're already dead." Not that it was worth arguing the point.

Tam indicated to the rest of us to wait outside the inn and disappeared inside then emerged a moment later with Callum behind him.

"Let's get out of here," said the werewolf.

"We're not going back to the inn?" Farley asked, confused. "Wait. Tam, *what* did you say to that guy?"

"I'll tell you on the way," he said. "We're going back to Grim Crag."

12

───────

"We're going *where*?" I hurried to catch up with Tam as he made for the path leading back to the sand dunes. "Hang on. We're not going to demand that Scarlet hand over the body, are we?"

"No," said Tam. "No, but we can make a proper plan on the way to the Crag."

"You set the inspector and the police up to argue with one another so they wouldn't stop us leaving?" I smothered a laugh. "What did you even say to him?"

"Whatever it was, the second-hand embarrassment made me want to bury my head in the sand dunes," said Farley. "Seriously, though, did you catch him out on the chimera licence thing?"

"Pretty much," Callum answered. "Tam got Kellen on the phone in two seconds flat. Turns out the office has never received any calls from the inspector, so I don't know who that guy thinks he's been calling for the past two days."

My brows shot up. "I knew he was crooked, but what does he have to gain from getting Lara's pet chimera taken away from her? Seems petty to me."

"It does," Tam agreed. "I still don't know what his reasoning is, but at least he's no longer in our way."

"Pity Lara had to take the fall," I said. "She did come to our rescue with the police."

"Kellen found proof of her licence registered with the Wardens," said Tam. "She'll be fine, but Inspector Peterson has some serious explaining to do to the head office."

"Couldn't have happened to a nicer guy." Callum sounded pleased enough that I suspected his questioning had been as pointless and infuriating as mine and Farley's had. "Though if she's innocent, and so is Alana, who *is* the killer?"

"I think the question we should be asking is 'what,' not 'who,'" Tam said. "I think our attention has been in the wrong place. Remember we usually deal with monsters, not people."

"Or monsters that look like people," I added. "Is that what you think it is? Something that looks like a person?"

"You think they've infiltrated the village of Grim Crag?" asked Farley. "You know, that does explain why nobody seems to have sighted anything weird in the area, if it's hiding among them."

Tam inclined his head. "Yes, and if we were in the company of a competent inspector who reported back to the office as he's supposed to, we might have been able to identify the real cause of the attacks sooner."

"That reminds me. I should text Kellen." I fumbled in my pocket for my phone as we walked. "I should have told him about Fenton's death."

"I told him earlier," Tam said. "He knows as much as we do."

"Or as little." I fished out my phone anyway. "Has he

checked the files for details on creatures that can block a vampire's mind-reading ability? It can't be that common."

"It isn't." Callum halted midstep. "You don't think someone is possessed, do you?"

My mouth parted. Somehow that possibility had slipped my mind, despite our previous case involving exactly that scenario. Granted, the demonic spirit in question had possessed a tree and not a person ... but the one who'd killed my predecessor had initially possessed her body and turned her against the others.

If someone in the village had been possessed, then it would certainly explain how the monster had gone undetected among their fellow villagers.

The colour drained from Farley's face. "If it's another demon, we don't need to worry about figuring out motives. They possess and kill people for the hell of it."

"We don't know for sure that's what we're dealing with," Callum said hastily. "It could be a creature that just *looks* like a person, like Perry and Tam said."

"Can demons block mind-reading abilities?" With my heart racing, I fired off a message to Kellen, asking him if any varieties of demonic spirit were known to bite or strangle their prey to death. As for blocking Maurice's mind-reading powers, that might be Scarlet's doing instead, but it was worth finding out.

"What're you doing?" asked Callum. "Asking Kellen for ideas?"

I slid my phone back into my pocket. "He might need to know more about the state of the bodies to figure it out."

"Going to the hospital to look at the tourists' bodies ourselves is certainly an option," Tam said, "but they might refuse entry to us on the grounds that we don't have the same authority as the inspector."

"As if he hasn't abused that authority to his own ends," I muttered. "What else are we supposed to do? Try to reason with Scarlet?"

"Looks that way," said Farley.

"Then we're trapped between a rock and a Grim Crag." Not my best one-liner, but the briefest of wry smiles touched Tam's lips, and my heart fluttered in response. "Want to put it to a vote?"

"I vote we talk to Scarlet," Callum said. "Granted, she might not be best pleased if we imply one of her people is possessed."

"No, but if I were her, I'd want to know," said Farley. "I'm with you. Maurice? I'm guessing you don't want to have Perry use another transportation charm on you to get to the hospital."

The vampire's jaw twitched. "No, but do we actually have a plan? I don't see Scarlet believing someone in her village is possessed without proof."

"If we walk slowly enough, Kellen might reply to my message before we get there." Not that we'd given him much to work with this time. I could tell the others weren't pleased with the uncertainty either, but short of returning to Herring Cove, we were low on options.

Kellen came to our rescue, and as I'd hoped, my phone buzzed with a reply within a few minutes.

Possession? It's possible, Kellen's message said. *If someone in the village is possessed, then there's a chance they aren't even aware.*

"That's what worried me," I said when I told the others his response.

Callum groaned. "That figures."

"How're we supposed to catch them out, then?" Maurice wanted to know.

"We've done it before," Tam reminded us. "We have a baseline to work with, and we already know how to handle monsters from the afterworld."

Did Scarlet or her coven, though? Most witches and wizards were only aware of the afterworld as a vague, abstract entity, not a haven for monsters. Besides, even if the poor soul playing host to a demon didn't know about the extra passenger sharing their body, there was still the question of who'd *summoned* the beast. Demons didn't just fall out of the sky.

That part would have to wait, but we might at least be able to delay Alana taking the fall for the monster's actions ... assuming we weren't already too late.

When we neared the village, I spotted someone sitting on a rock some distance away from the houses. At first, I thought it was Walter and made to warn the others, but then I recognised Charles, Fenton's friend. His ragged clothes were soaked through with rain and seawater, and he was perched on the edge of the rock, staring into the distance.

Tam approached him. "Charles?"

He blinked at us as if awakening from a trance. "You again? Didn't you just leave?"

"We did, but we're back," said Tam. "What are you doing out here?"

"I don't know." He sighed. "I can't help thinking I should have been able to save him."

"Fenton?" Come to think of it, hadn't Charles been the last person who'd seen Fenton before his death? I hadn't wanted to interrogate him earlier, but since we were here, I figured I might as well ask him a couple of questions while Scarlet and her coven weren't hovering over our shoulders. "You went to meet him this morning. Was anyone else awake at that time?"

"Huh?" He pushed off the rock and onto his feet. "I don't know."

The storm had blown itself out not long before dawn, as far as I knew. Nobody would have been outside in the pouring rain, possessed or otherwise, but after?

"Charles, when you went to meet Fenton, do you remember seeing or hearing anything odd?" I asked.

"What?" he asked, his voice strained. "I don't know what you mean."

"What do you remember?" I pressed. "It might be important. Were you the only person outside when you went to meet him?"

"Was I?" His voice dropped to a whisper. "I don't know. I don't know."

I might have put the distress in his voice down to grief, but his evident confusion coupled with his shifty manner nagged at me like an itch.

"Charles, do you have any ... any gaps in your memory?"

At my question, his mouth hung open for a second. Then his eyes turned a sharp, flat black colour, and he *moved*, faster than any person should be able to, sprinting down the path as if pursued by a rabid manticore.

"Whoa." I took a step back. "What the—?"

Maurice whipped around, his fangs exposed. "Way to scare off our target."

"We didn't know he was the target until the literal second he ran off," I pointed out, but Maurice had already vanished in pursuit. Good job, because I wouldn't have had a chance of catching up to Charles while he was running full tilt across the clifftops towards the beach.

"He's not a vampire, is he?" Callum stared after Maurice and Charles. "How can he move that fast?"

"He's possessed." Tam's hand strayed towards his jacket

pocket, in which I assumed he'd concealed a weapon or two. "He must have felt threatened and fled … or should I say the creature possessing him felt threatened."

"I didn't expect him to freak out like that." I pulled out my wand, for all the good it did, and watched Maurice close in on Charles from behind. "I really didn't know it was him. Not until I saw how weird he was acting."

"What are you doing?" asked a familiar voice. "What's your friend doing to Charles?"

I suppressed a groan. Walter approached us from behind, his attention on Maurice. The vampire had managed to grab Charles and sling him over one shoulder to carry him back uphill to the village.

"Walter, I'd appreciate it if you fetched Scarlet," said Tam. "Immediately."

He didn't move until Maurice reappeared with Charles in tow. The villager struggled feebly, but the vampire's iron grip held tight.

"What do you want me to do with him?" Maurice asked. "Shake him until the monster falls out?"

"Monster?" Walter stared. "What are you talking about?"

"Charles is possessed," I explained. "By the same creature that killed Fenton and those two tourists."

"Possessed?"

Charles moaned, prompting Maurice to tighten his hold, and the same odd blackness appeared in Charles's eyes again as he struggled to escape.

"He might not be the only one," said the vampire. "Did anyone think of that?"

Good point. "We need to tell Scarlet—didn't you hear Tam ask you to fetch her?" I directed this at Walter. "Make yourself useful for once. Go on."

Instead of listening to me, Walter reached into his pocket.

"Wait!" Tam stepped in, but Walter had already pulled out his wand and pointed it directly at Charles.

A loud bang went off, and Maurice released Charles a heartbeat before the spell hit the villager square in the chest. Charles staggered back, and a blur of darkness surged out of his body. *A demon.* The darkness coalesced on the path in front of us, surged uphill, and vanished as swiftly as the vampire had.

"Thanks a bunch," I said to Walter. "Now it's free to possess someone else."

I looked wildly around, but the creature was long gone. Recovering from his shock, Walter took a step towards Charles's limp form. The villager lay unconscious on the path, and I only hoped the spell Walter had used on him hadn't caused any permanent damage.

"What are you doing?" I demanded when he reached for Charles's body. Had he not seen the demon escape? Granted, not everyone could see ghosts or spirits, but still.

"I'd like to know that myself." Scarlet strode into view, her own wand in her hand. "Stirring up trouble again, are you?"

"Charles was possessed," Tam told her. "The creature released him and escaped into the village."

"It's true," said Walter. "I removed the creature from his body myself, but I believe ... I believe we've found the person responsible for murdering Fenton."

Scarlet stared at him for a moment, her expression unreadable. Then she moved over to Charles and levitated his body into the air with a flick of her wand.

"Hang on," I said. "He might not even know he was possessed. And the creature is still out there."

"If he's a murderer, then he'll face the extent of the law." She gave another flick of her wand, propelling him down the main road through the village. *Not this again.* For all I knew, the creature had possessed *her* next, but I wouldn't have been able to tell either way. It was the demonic tree all over again—but with people instead and ones who refused to listen to a word we said.

"Does that mean you're letting Alana go?" I asked Scarlet.

Without turning back, she said, "Alana will still be questioned. This doesn't change the crime she committed."

I hurried after her. "And Charles? Locking him in jail won't stop the creature from possessing him again. A locked door is no barrier to a spirit."

"All the more reason to see to it that he is contained."

"He might not even remember what he did or why he was locked up," I protested. "What if the creature chooses a different host, or if there's more than one? Did you plan to lock up half the village?"

Scarlet didn't answer. Several coven members had come out of their headquarters to see what the fuss was about and stared at Charles's unconscious body hovering at their leader's side.

"I've found our murderer." Scarlet raised her voice to address everyone in the region. "Charles has been found to be possessed by an unknown entity that used his body to kill Fenton. We must secure him at once."

Panicked whispers broke out among the other witches while I tried and failed to see if any of their number was the demon's new host. I hadn't a hope of identifying them without a sign like the creepy blackness that had suffused Charles's eyes when I'd exposed him, and when I glanced over my shoulder, I spotted Tam beckoning me back to join him and the others.

I strode back to the rest of the team. "We have to draw that thing out. What if it kills again?"

"It won't," Tam said. "Not yet. From the way Charles fled when he was exposed, I'm guessing it's afraid of taking on our entire team. When you add the coven on top of that, I imagine it'll plan to lie low."

"You could have waited before cornering him," said Maurice. "Now it's too late."

"Waited?" I echoed. "I didn't corner him. I asked him a question. Besides, that Walter guy is the one who knocked him out cold. He doesn't seem to care that Scarlet's arrested the wrong person *again*."

"I don't know that he's the wrong person," said Callum. "I mean, what if he's the guy who summoned the beast to begin with?"

"We're still missing a motive." I turned to Tam. "We can't leave the villagers to handle this alone. I know they aren't undefended, but I doubt they have experience dealing with possession. We need to help them."

"The beast won't expose itself again easily," Tam said. "That said—we certainly shouldn't be splitting up at a time like this."

"Huh?" I spun back to the others and saw that Maurice had vanished. "Oh, for crying out loud. Where's he gone?"

"I don't know," said Farley, "but we never did find out why he can't use his powers in Grim Crag. It must be driving him out of his mind."

Tam muttered a curse. "I'll find him. You three wait here. I don't need to reiterate why none of you should wander off alone with that creature out there, do I?"

Farley let out a quiet noise, while Callum moved protectively to her side.

"This isn't like that," he said. "It won't be."

My heart contracted when Tam turned away, though not before I saw a similar glint of grief and distress in his eyes. Witnessing their shared pain, I felt for a moment what it might be to be an empath like Farley.

"No," I said. "It won't be like that. We'll stop it first."

"How—" Farley gave a choked noise, and I realised I'd given entirely too much away about my knowledge of the details of Clarice's death. Kellen had told me in confidence after I'd asked in an effort to understand my team better, but I'd little expected to be thrown into a similar mission so soon after our first.

Had the office known? Had the *inspector*? Call me paranoid, but the Wardens were hardly ignorant of the circumstances of my predecessor's death, and the inspector had brought up the subject enough times for me to wonder if he'd known the similarities between the cases all along. And he hadn't told us.

Whatever his agenda was, we had bigger problems on our hands, and Maurice's newest disappearing act was the least of them. Scarlet had jailed the wrong person yet again, and if the creature *did* come back for its host, then she might just have given the demon's summoner exactly what they wanted.

13

———

While we waited for Tam to return, the others were silent for several moments before someone addressed the elephant in the room.

"You knew," Farley said quietly. "Who told you? Tam would never."

My face heated. "Kellen did, because I asked. I wanted to make sure I didn't accidentally touch on any sore subjects in the future. I didn't know our next mission might end up involving something similar."

Callum exhaled. "I guess it had to come out eventually."

"It's unfair." Farley turned away, her eyes glittering with tears. "That inspector decided to bring it up during my questioning too. If I didn't know better, I'd say he was baiting us on purpose."

I wasn't the only one who thought the timing was suspicious, then. "What if he *did* know? What...?" I saw someone approaching from the direction of the sand dunes. "Speak of the devil."

"What's he doing out here?" Callum eyed the inspector's oncoming figure.

"Finally doing his job?" Whatever the case, the idea of explaining how the monster had escaped on our watch would be about as fun as diving off the cliffs into the ice-cold water. "We should probably warn him there's an invisible monster on the loose. Without implying we were responsible for its escape."

"I doubt we're going to pass the inspection at this point," Farley said.

She wasn't wrong, but I couldn't believe he'd actually left Herring Cove and walked all the way up here. He reached the top of the slope, his face flushed, but he was hardly out of breath from the steep climb, and he glared at us. "I don't remember giving you permission to come back here."

"We had a killer to find." I should have guessed he'd be angry that Tam had led us out of the village while he'd been occupied, but it was his own fault for trying to get Lara and her chimera into trouble instead of helping with the murder investigation.

"Inspector." Tam walked uphill to join us, accompanied by a surly-looking Maurice. "We found the demonic spirit responsible for the murders, which had been possessing one of the citizens of Grim Crag. Unfortunately, while we found its host, the spirit escaped before we could banish it from this realm."

The colour drained from the inspector's face. "You found the beast responsible for the deaths, and you let it get away?"

"The villagers took matters into their own hands and let it escape," I corrected him. "Then they arrested the man who was being possessed. I believe the spirit is still hiding in the area, so we could use your help flushing it out."

"Certainly not," he said. "You will all come back to the inn with me at once."

"We're on a mission," Tam said. "It's out of the question for us to leave the villagers with a dangerous monster potentially hiding among them, waiting to strike again."

"It sounds as if they're capable of handling it themselves," he said. "A demonic spirit, is it? That ought to be easy enough to banish."

"You can't know that." Was he serious? "Would you stake innocent lives on it? Look, there's a time and a place for procedure, and this isn't it."

"That's for me to decide." He beckoned pointedly to our group. "If you refuse to obey my orders one more time, then I will have to report your team to the office. They'll take steps, especially concerning those of you who seem to be unable to follow the Wardens' rules."

My mouth fell open, and the others looked stunned, even Tam. None of us could argue with such a direct threat, so we left Grim Crag behind and retraced our steps to Herring Cove. My energy levels were seriously starting to flag by this point, telling me it was far past lunchtime, which meant we had an ever-decreasing number of hours until the sun began to go down.

Then the beast might go out to feed again.

I hope it gets the inspector next time. That was unlikely, given that he'd only come to the village to fetch the rest of us, not to speak to Scarlet or the coven, as if we were disobedient children who'd sneaked out on his watch. It gave little comfort that the others shared in my fury. Farley's hands were shaking at her sides, Callum's mouth was set in a grim line, and even Maurice showed no signs of his usual indifference. No doubt he could read the inspector's mind and see exactly how serious he was about his threats. Meanwhile, though Tam's face revealed no hints of anger, the quiet calmness of his expression didn't quite conceal a simmering rage.

If I were the inspector, I'd be running for the hills, but he barely looked at us on our way through the village. Inspector Peterson led us directly to the inn without stopping at the police station. Presumably that meant he'd cleared up matters with the Phils, though I couldn't see whether Lara was still inside the office or not. If the Wardens' office had backed her up on the chimera licence issue, they'd have had to give in, and I had little doubt that the inspector's current rampage was intended as payback for the way Tam had exposed his failings.

The inspector wanted to remind all of us of his authority, and if we disobeyed, we'd lose everything. Or some of us would. As the team's newest member and the target of his ire, I had little doubt that he'd see to it that I faced the brunt of the punishment in the form of being kicked off the team or worse.

Kellen would back me up, I was sure, but any delay to the mission risked another victim being claimed by the beast in Grim Crag, and their deaths would be on the inspector's conscience—if he had one, which I doubted.

Once he'd hauled us into the dining room at the inn, Inspector Peterson snapped at the owner to leave us alone and launched into a diatribe on the subject of our disobedience. I tuned him out after the first wave of insults, but it was difficult to ignore the effect on Farley. She'd sunk back in her seat, tears streaming down her face.

Glancing at her, Tam said, "As team leader, I take full responsibility for my team's actions. I would request to speak to you alone, as is appropriate in these cases."

The inspector glowered at the rest of us. "In that case,

the rest of the team shall wait upstairs in the dormitories. They aren't off the hook yet."

Leaving Tam to the wolves didn't appeal, but Farley jumped to her feet and fled the room, followed shortly by Maurice. That left it to Callum and me to find them, but when we reached the lobby, the vampire had already gone.

"Tam said not to split up," I muttered ineffectually.

Callum caught up to Farley at the stairs and put an arm around her, and I let them walk ahead of me. While they disappeared upstairs, muffled yelling came from the closed door to the dining room. My hands curled into fists. Tam didn't deserve to bear the brunt of the inspector's wrath, but even if I called Kellen, he could hardly trek all the way up here to come to our rescue.

As I hovered in the lobby, debating whether to leap in and potentially make matters worse, the inn's front door opened, and Lara, of all people, walked in.

"What—what are you doing here?" I spoke in a whisper, conscious of the closed door to the dining room, but the inspector's muffled yelling continued uninterrupted.

"Looking for you." She shot an alarmed look at the closed door. "I saw you were back, but … what's going on in there?"

"If you want to talk, we'd better go upstairs," I whispered. "The inspector has ordered us to go back to our rooms like grounded teenagers."

"Ouch." As a particularly loud yell came from the restaurant, she hastened to climb the stairs behind me.

At the top, the door to the boys' dorm was slightly ajar. Inside, I glimpsed Farley sobbing into Callum's shoulder, so I left them to their privacy and led Lara down to the girls' dorm room.

When I closed the door behind us, Lara gave me a questioning look. "What's your boss all riled up about? That you left the village without his permission?"

"Pretty much." Farley's empath abilities weren't my secret to share, and neither were the similarities between this case and the one that had ended in my predecessor's death. "He's been wanting to tear into us for a while, though."

"Because of me." She lowered her gaze. "I didn't mean to give you guys so much trouble."

"No, it's more our fault than yours. You did everything by the book." I paused, debating, then figured it couldn't hurt to give her a little more information. "We didn't, and now he's got us under house arrest while the monster that killed three people is loose in Grim Crag."

"You *found* the monster?" Her eyes rounded. "And he let it go?"

"He thinks Scarlet and the others can handle the beast themselves, which might be true, but it's capable of possessing any villager without them being aware of its presence."

"Possessing?" Her brows shot up. "What? Like a ghost?"

"More or less," I said. "It's a demonic spirit, I think, but I only got a glimpse of it. When we found the guy who was possessed, it ran off rather than fight our entire team."

"Does Scarlet know?"

"Yeah, but she arrested the guy who got possessed instead of going after the demon." I shook my head. "The monster is lying low, I think, but I don't see it leaving the village that easily."

"So, it's likely to choose another host." She pursed her lips. "Is there anything I can do to help?"

"I could use another diversion," I said. "No, not really.

The more trouble we get into, the more hassle my supervisor has to deal with to get us out of it."

"Your supervisor? Not that guy downstairs?"

"Not him, no." I reached for my phone and pulled up Kellen's latest message. "Kellen is on our side, unlike the inspector, but he's miles away from here. It'll take too long to bring him in to get that guy to simmer down so we can deal with the case without him getting underfoot."

"Tricky," she said. "That guy has a screw loose. You know, when he showed up and started asking me questions about Cupcake, it seemed official enough. I showed him the paperwork and thought that was the end of it, but then the police called and started asking questions too. Next thing you know, my licence is missing. The Wardens found the online registration and said they'd send me a replacement, but ... is it bad that I don't entirely trust them?"

"I don't blame you," I said. "He has some nerve lecturing *us* about not following procedure, but we're the ones who'll take the fall."

And so would the people of Grim Crag if the monster killed again.

She sucked in a breath. "If you meant what you said about a diversion, let me know if you want me to bring Cupcake to frighten that inspector of yours. He might have no teeth, but he can roar loudly enough to give anyone a scare."

"I don't want you getting into trouble again." I pulled up Kellen's number, figuring it wouldn't take long to make the call, and with the inspector occupied with Tam, I wouldn't get a better chance than this. "I'm going to call my supervisor. He might be able to pull off a miracle and get here before someone else dies." Man, that was depressing.

"Screw getting into trouble." Lara's face was set. "If lives are at risk, I'm more than happy to cause all the diversions you need."

"If you're sure, wait until I'm done calling Kellen."

"Cupcake will be thrilled. I never let him out during the day." She made for the door and opened it. "Give it, say, half an hour?"

"Sure." I managed a half smile. "Thanks."

"Good luck."

Once she'd left, I called Kellen at the office, and he picked up right away.

"Perry," he said. "I wondered if I might hear from you."

"Yeah," I murmured. "Did you guess we'd end up in even more trouble?"

"I hoped *not*," said Kellen, "but I worried that Inspector Peterson might take out his anger on you after the incident with the chimera licence."

"That's the least of it." I took in a breath and told him about the incident with the demonic spirit. "It's hiding among the people of Grim Crag, looking for someone else to possess, and I'd wager that we don't have much time before it picks another host."

He swore under his breath. "If you tell him *that,* he can't hold you hostage. Are you at ... what's it called? Herring Cove?"

"Yes. He has us confined to our rooms, except Tam, whom he's still yelling at."

He swore again. "If he thinks you aren't doing your jobs, then it's one thing, but he's—"

"Preventing us from doing our jobs himself. I know," I interjected. "I know I'm not in a place to argue against a superior, but he's going against procedure himself in the way he's behaving towards us. He seems to have a personal grudge against me, and on the first day, he made a point of comparing me to my predecessor. That's not exactly professional and impartial, is it?"

"No," he said. "It isn't. Your predecessor? Really?"

"Yeah." I kept my voice lower in the hopes that Farley and Callum wouldn't be able to hear us. "This case... The fact that it involves someone who's possessed seems almost designed to bring up bad memories with the others too."

"That can't be possible," he said. "The case wasn't registered as a possession. We sent you in because we didn't know what was going on over there."

But did the inspector? Had he feigned ignorance from the start? "I'm just saying it feels like we walked right into a trap."

"Your last mission involved possession, didn't it?" he reminded me. "I know it's a sore subject with the others, but there's a limited number of Wardens with the specific skillset you need to deal with demonic spirits. In any case... Wait, do the others know you're aware of how Clarice died?"

"I had to tell them." I closed my eyes. "Sorry, Kellen. I made it clear that I'm the one who asked you to tell me the details, but ... the inspector knew too. I'm sure he did."

He was silent for a moment. "I can raise enquiries within the department, but that won't help with your current dilemma. For a start, we need to identify the type of spirit you're dealing with. How does it kill?"

"That, I'm not sure of," I said. "Tam said the victims looked as if they'd been strangled, but he wasn't sure. The official reports said they drowned."

"Draining life force," he muttered. "Yes ... that sounds like a Class Two or Three demonic spirit."

"Draining *what*?"

"Higher-class demons literally suck the life out of their victims simply by touching them," Kellen elaborated. "It wouldn't leave much of a mark. I'd guess the bite marks and signs of strangulation came from the victim trying to fight the demon off."

"Yeah. That makes sense." My throat closed up at the memory of Charles's confused grief at the sight of Fenton's body. "I need to tell Scarlet. That reminds me, Maurice said he can't read anyone's mind in Grim Crag. Is that likely to be the spirit's doing?"

"Yes," he said, "but it's usually restricted to the possessed individual, whose mind cannot be penetrated by a vampire's abilities."

"Wait. So it shouldn't affect everyone else in the area?"

"Not unless he's spent an extensive amount of time around the individual in question."

Chills raced down my arms. "He hasn't. Kellen ... what does that mean?"

No reply.

"Kellen?"

"Let me look into it," he said quietly. "I don't like the implications, but I think we're dealing with more than one spirit. I also think that this situation merits bypassing the traditional route of taking instruction from your immediate supervisor."

My heart missed a beat. "You're giving me permission to ignore the inspector and act on your orders instead?"

"I'm giving all of you permission, but please try not to break too many rules. Within reason."

"Got it." A grin swept over my mouth briefly before my heart began racing again. How on earth were we supposed to get out of here without a violent altercation? The inspector might be the hands-off type, but that didn't mean he couldn't hold his own in a fight.

"Good luck." Kellen ended the call, and I slid my phone

back into my pocket and then walked down the corridor to the boys' dorm.

I nudged the door open. Farley had stopped crying, but both she and Callum looked warily at me when I slipped into the room.

"Hey," I whispered. "So ... I have good news and bad news."

I summarised my call with Kellen as quickly as possible, adding that Lara had offered to help us.

When I'd finished, Farley spoke first. "We have permission to go out again without asking the inspector, but we still don't have an actual plan for dealing with this spirit. *Multiple* spirits, potentially. Are you sure we should be in a hurry to leave?"

"Multiple spirits that feed on souls," Callum added. "Or life force or whatever it is."

"That's why they don't leave any obvious wounds on their targets' bodies."

My phone buzzed with a message from Kellen.

"Ah—he said he forgot to mention during our call that however many spirits there are, they were likely summoned by a single person."

Farley sank back onto the bed. "I don't like this. I don't like it at all."

"Neither do I, but we're in too deep to back out now," Callum said, "and we need to stick together. I hope Maurice didn't go far, but vampires can't be possessed."

"Lucky him," I said sourly. "We need to rescue Tam, first and foremost. I don't know what we'll do if the inspector refuses to let him go, though. Kellen told me not to break any other rules, if I can help it."

"That means we can't beat him up," said Callum. "More's the pity."

"There are other ways," I said. "We can lock him in a cupboard."

"Or tell him there's another monster on the loose," Callum suggested.

"That reminds me, Lara offered to bring Cupcake here to create a diversion."

Farley snorted. "That might land her in trouble again, but I doubt the inspector would try to fight a chimera single-handedly."

"Or us." Callum cracked his knuckles. "Poor Kellen's going to be stuck with most of the paperwork after this, but we'll worry about the inspector once we've dealt with the monster."

"And whether Scarlet likes it or not, we're coming to help her."

I led the way out of the dormitory and downstairs. The creaky old stairs announced our presence, and when I reached the lobby, I could no longer hear any shouting from behind the closed door. The inspector had heard us.

Bracing myself, I approached the door a moment before it opened, and the inspector's furious face appeared. "I told you to go back to your rooms."

"I've just had an urgent call from the office pertaining to the mission." I cut through his objections. "I have permission from my supervisor for the entire team to take action against the beast attacking the people of Grim Crag without need to ask another figure of authority."

Inspector Peterson's face flushed an even deeper red than before. "That's not allowed. You can't do that."

"She can." Tam somehow managed to manoeuvre his way around the inspector and out into the lobby. "In an emergency. This situation certainly qualifies as such."

"Exactly," I said, and Callum and Farley nodded in

agreement. "The usual procedures are on hold. If you have a problem, call the office."

"I won't have this," he said. "None of you is to move an inch."

A rumbling growl came from outside, raising the hairs on my arms. The inspector took a startled step backwards then another, and Callum lunged for the dining room door. When the door closed on the startled inspector, Farley stepped forward with her wand in her hand. Sparks flew left and right, but the locking charm that hit the door was perfectly cast.

"Nicely done," Tam breathed. "That won't hold him for long."

"It's enough." I ran for the door, where I found Lara holding on to her chimera's lead, struggling to restrain him.

"I wasn't too early, was I?" she asked.

"No, you got here just in time." I glanced over my shoulder at the inn. "The inspector's locked up but not for long. We need to go."

"Then I'll come with you. Seems safer."

I raised a brow. "Safer to be around a horde of demonic spirits?"

"A horde of spirits?" Tam echoed. "Perry, tell me everything."

I relayed my chat with Kellen to him while we walked towards the sand dunes. Partway there, Maurice reappeared, so I had to repeat the whole thing again. At least he hadn't wandered far, so the whole team was ready.

"Scarlet and her entire coven are playing host to a bunch of demons?" he said. "Yeah, I can see that."

"I don't know that they're *all* possessed, but enough of them are to affect your mind-reading abilities," I said.

"Besides, don't forget that not all of them will be aware of the extra passenger sharing their body."

"Except whoever summoned them," Tam added. "The good news is that they can all be dealt with using a regular banishment spell, once we have them cornered."

"What if they outnumber us?" asked Farley. "I don't like those odds."

"It won't be the entire village," I said. "For a start, vampires can't be possessed, which counts Alana out."

Maurice made a sceptical noise. "She's locked up."

"Not for long, I'm betting," I said. "You of all people ought to know how hard it is to keep a vampire contained."

"Wait a moment," said Callum. "If almost everyone in the village is possessed, wouldn't there be more signs? Even if they don't need to feed every day, there's only been three victims."

"Good point," I said. "Kellen said that most vampires would only be affected if they spent a lot of time around the possessed person, but I'd say there are two or three of them at most."

That was worse than one but better than a dozen.

"What did Kellen mean by 'a lot of time'?" Maurice's eyes narrowed. "I hardly spent any time in that ghastly village."

"We'll revisit that one later." I had my suspicions, but at least one demonic spirit lurked among the villagers, and there was no telling whether they'd go after another victim tonight or not.

And if they did, nobody would be safe. We had to end this.

14

We made an odd group, walking back to Grim Crag with the chimera in tow. Once one got past his alarming appearance, Cupcake was pretty docile, letting Lara lead him along without complaint.

"Are you sure you want to bring him with us?"

"Cupcake is safer outside the village for the time being," she said. "He can't be possessed, and he's not useless in a fight either."

If nothing else, I supposed he might be able to give Scarlet and her coven a scare if she tried to drive us off—assuming she wasn't one of the possessed villagers. We had to face it—there was no way to tell who played host to a demon until they exposed themselves.

"What's the plan, then?" asked Callum. "We can't banish the demons until they let go of their hosts, which would be less of an issue if we knew who they were possessing."

"The last one let go of its host when that Walter hit him with a spell," I said. "We can't do that to every villager, though."

"Can't we?" Maurice bared his teeth. "We can give them a scare and see if it lures the demons out of hiding."

I rolled my eyes at him. "It might, but then they'd run off again, wouldn't they?"

"Unless we set a trap," said Maurice.

"You mean a circle of sage?" I looked at the others. "Does anyone have any sage?"

"We don't," said Callum. "Unless someone wants to volunteer to fly back to the tower and fetch some."

"We don't have time," Farley said. "This isn't looking like much of a plan, to be honest."

"Better than staying in our rooms on the inspector's orders." I racked my brain, trying to think of any other way to trap the demons for long enough to cast a banishment spell. "Right. If we don't have sage, we'll have to find another way to corner the demonic spirit and then banish it."

"We?" Maurice raised a brow. "I thought you were the only person on the team who could cast a banishment spell. What're the rest of us supposed to do?"

"You're the one who's immune to possession," I pointed out. "That means you're the only one of us who can get right up close to the spirit without being harmed."

"What do you want me to do? Catch the host and shake them until the monster falls out?"

"Might work," Callum said. "Try not to hurt the host too much, though. We don't need to get into trouble for using excessive force."

"Shame," said Maurice. "If you ask me, we're already in deep-enough trouble that it can hardly hurt."

"We need Scarlet's cooperation, which she won't give us if we attack her people," I said. "Granted, I'm working on the assumption that she isn't one of the possessed villagers herself."

"She probably isn't," said Tam. "A coven leader is high-profile enough that someone would have noticed."

"That, and the monster attacked a member of their own community," said Callum. "Charles's only friend seemed to be Fenton, and he wasn't exactly all there. It's no surprise nobody caught him out."

"She might not be possessed, but she's done nothing but get in our way or arrest the wrong people," said Maurice. "I vote we keep her out of our plans."

"Don't forget we still need to catch whoever summoned the demons in the first place," said Tam. "They're the real masterminds, not the people who are currently possessed."

"Unless they're one and the same." Our theories were as full of holes as our plan, which was more of a string of last resorts than anything else. Without the inspector or the coven's cooperation, our only option was to draw out the creature on our own and hope that nobody else paid the price for it.

"So, we have two people who can't be possessed," Callum said. "Maurice and the chimera, if he counts as a person."

"Don't let him hear you say that," Lara reprimanded him. "That doesn't mean I'm willing to let the villagers *or* the demon use him as target practice."

"Understandable," Tam said. "Also, I know he's immune to being possessed, but you aren't."

"I still want to help," said Lara. "Just to make it clear."

"Can you create another diversion?" I queried. "Not if it puts Cupcake in danger, but if the villagers think they're under attack, then the spirits might come out into the open."

"And into your trap?" she asked. "Might work, but I'm a

middling witch, at best. I can't beat a coven leader like Scarlet in open combat."

"I can," said Maurice. "It'd be easier if I could read her thoughts, but if necessary…"

"Let's not get ahead of ourselves." We needed to focus on the monster, not the villagers. "Actually, we have three people who can't be possessed, if you count Alana…"

"I told you, we can't count her in," Maurice said. "She's in jail, and what makes you think she'll volunteer to help us anyway? Unless you want to break her out of the witches' jail, but that sounds like an unnecessary diversion."

"What is it, Perry?" asked Tam, eyeing me. "You thought of something, didn't you?"

"I think I figured out where we can find some sage," I said. "Alana's house is full of herbs and ingredients, and since vampires can't be possessed, it doesn't matter if we borrow them."

"Yes," said Callum. "Yes—perfect."

"You want to break into her house while she's in jail?" asked Maurice.

"Since when did you develop a conscience?" I rolled my eyes. "She'd give us permission if she knew, and we need that sage more than she does. So do the other villagers."

I looked at Tam, and my heart skipped a beat when I saw the approval in his eyes.

"Yes." He nodded. "One of us can go into her house and fetch the sage while the others keep an eye out for Scarlet and her coven. Lara, you and the chimera can wait outside the town … we'll keep the diversion idea on hold until we've had time to set up a trap for the demons."

"I don't think the coven's out." The village was too quiet for them to be roaming the streets, so they must have returned to their headquarters. It was Walter who might be lurking around, waiting to ruin our plans, intentionally or not, so I kept both eyes open for him while Callum volunteered to go into Alana's house.

The rest of us waited with bated breath until Callum emerged from Alana's home with a bag of sage in his hands. "I had to go through her cabinets to find it. I think it's safe to say *she* didn't know there was a beast from the afterworld in the village."

That proved beyond all shadow of a doubt that she was innocent of involvement in the demon's summoning—not that that was Scarlet's biggest concern.

"Where do you want to set up the circle?" I asked.

"There's only one street," said Callum. "If we block off the end, it doesn't mean it won't flee elsewhere, but I don't see it going out to sea. It won't find anyone to possess out there."

"Yeah ... set it up here." I gestured to the dirt path beneath our feet. "Maybe set up a second one at the other end of the street too."

"I will." Maurice held out a hand for the bag of sage. "I can move faster, and it'll give me the chance to see if anyone's lurking around."

"Good call." Tam watched him leave, while Cupcake growled.

"What is it?" I spun back to Lara. "Can he sense the demon?"

"No, he's not comfortable being around so many people," she said as Cupcake growled again. I didn't blame him for being on edge, but if we weren't careful, the noise would draw attention.

As Callum finished setting up a circle of sage across the end of the road, Lara gave a gentle tug on the chimera's lead. "Come on, Cupcake. Let's move."

The chimera didn't budge. Lara strained to drag him out of sight, but attempting to wrestle a giant lion-alligator hybrid who didn't want to move was an exercise in futility. Worse, I heard the unmistakeable creak of a door opening further up the street.

"Someone's coming," I muttered to the others. "If it's the demon, we need to be ready."

"Come *on,* Cupcake." With difficulty, Lara dragged the chimera off the path and out of view of the houses, while I walked down the street to face the person who'd come outside—namely the poodle lady, which was an improvement on Walter, if nothing else.

"What are you doing?" Her gaze went to the bag of sage in Callum's hands. "Are you casting a spell on us?"

"No, we're setting up a trap for that demonic spirit," I told her.

A growl came from behind the houses, and she jumped. "What was that?"

I thought fast. "We have, ah, a backup team ready to fight the demon if it escapes. Where's Scarlet?"

"In the coven's headquarters. Where else?" At another, louder growl, she jumped violently. "What have you brought here?"

Further down the street, the doors to the coven's head-quarters opened. When Scarlet emerged, the poodle lady fled to her side.

"*They* brought something dangerous here." She jabbed an accusing finger in our direction. "We're under attack."

"Hold on." I should have guessed she'd jump to the worst possible conclusion. "I told you, we brought reinforce-ments to help you get rid of the demonic spirit that's on the loose near your village—"

"What was that noise?" she demanded. "Did you bring another monster to fight off this one?"

"He won't hurt any humans," Callum told her. "He's here to scare that creature out into the open. He doesn't even have any teeth."

Cupcake chose that moment to prowl back into view, dragging Lara behind him. Upon seeing Scarlet and the others, she attempted a reassuring smile. "Sorry, he's nervous around new people."

"That's a demon!" one of the witches exclaimed, pointing at the chimera.

"No, he isn't," Lara protested, but the chimera's ensuing growl did not inspire confidence. "We're here to help you."

Scarlet exchanged words with a couple of her fellow coven members and then marched over to our group, her wand in her hand. "We didn't give you permission to help us, let alone by bringing a dangerous predator to our community."

"His bark is worse than his bite, literally." My words went unheard when a bone-chilling howl arose from somewhere within the village. "That wasn't the chimera."

Had the demon finally shown itself? I reached for my wand, and when a second howl arose from the direction of the seafront, panic erupted among the coven members. Some fled, others drew their wands, and when a loud thump sounded, everyone surged towards the witches' headquarters.

This time, Maurice emerged from the building, carrying Charles's body over his shoulder. *What? When did he get in there?*

In a blink, the vampire was at our side and had tossed the older man into the circle of sage at the street's end.

"He's possessed," he said to a scandalised Scarlet and her coven members. "Watch."

Charles lifted his head and let out a chilling howl, which drew another panicked snarl from the chimera. As we watched, a blur of darkness detached itself from Charles's body for the second time—only to come to a halt when it met the boundary of the circle of sage. The patch of darkness surged around the edges of the circle, unable to escape.

"It's trapped." Ignoring the terrified murmurs from the coven members behind me, I approached the circle of sage. "Anyone else here know how to use a banishing spell? If not, stand back."

I didn't wait for a reply. Pointing my wand at the demonic spirit, I whispered the words I'd learned in training to deal with beasts from the afterworld. *Get out of here.*

Light surged from my wand, blanketing the patch of darkness, and when it cleared, the beast was gone. In the ensuing shocked silence, Scarlet came marching past. "If you don't mind, I'd like to have my prisoner back."

"Hang on," I said. "He might not have known he was possessed. I told you before."

"I think you're forgetting something more important," Maurice said. "Who *summoned* that creature? Who in this village has knowledge of dark magic?"

"Nobody." Scarlet sounded affronted. "Nobody does."

"Someone summoned that creature," I said. "In fact, they summoned more than one."

Wherever the other spirits were hiding, they hadn't shown their faces yet. How do we draw them out?

"Yes," said Maurice through gritted teeth. "They did."

From his tone, I gathered that he still couldn't read the villagers' minds. There must be at least one spirit hiding among the people of Grim Crag, if not more.

"What are you implying?" Scarlet asked. "More than one spirit? What would give you that idea?"

"Trust me. We know," I said. "This is our area of expertise. Also, if I were you, I'd let Alana out of jail."

"And why exactly would I do that?"

"Because vampires can't be possessed," I explained. "We're going to need all the allies we can get."

"Alana lied to us," said Scarlet. "She is no ally, and neither is this man." She gestured to Charles, who'd slumped into a moaning heap on the path.

"Does he look like a threat to you or anyone else?" I scanned the coven members, but they hadn't come any closer, as if they were reluctant to come near the circle of sage. There was no way for me to tell if any of *them* were possessed.

"Hey, Lara," Callum said in an undertone. "Can your pet scare the remaining spirit into letting go of its host?"

The chimera, however, had slunk out of sight. Lara stuck her head around the corner from a nearby house. "He's gone shy. Too many strangers."

"Unless someone has an alternative, he's going to have to get over it." I looked at Scarlet, who glowered at me.

"I refuse to let you bring that monster any closer to our community," she said. "It's dangerous."

"The chimera doesn't have any teeth," I told her. "Listen —someone else here is possessed. Maybe more than one person. We're not safe yet."

As for whoever had summoned the beasts ... well, that was another issue altogether. We'd have to deal with that one later, because it was clear Scarlet wasn't going to listen to us as long as the chimera remained within sniffing distance of the village.

Scarlet reached for Charles, only to release him when

the chimera let out an ear-splitting roar. *What is it this time?* Looking wildly around in case a second demon had resurfaced, I instead saw Walter sprinting down the street, where he stopped short at the sight of our group. "What is going on here?"

Someone screamed, cutting off Scarlet's answer. The coven members scattered yet again when a woman sprinted from their headquarters, her cloak flying behind her and her eyes flat black. *There's our second demon.*

I nodded to Maurice. "Do the honours?"

The woman attempted to flee, but as Maurice prepared to grab her, Walter got in her way first. The possessed woman ducked around him, while Scarlet shouted orders to the other witches. Spells collided in mid-air, all of them missing their target, who darted in and out of sight at speed. When Walter took aim with his own wand, Maurice tackled him off his feet.

"How dare you!" Walter spluttered to thin air. The vampire, of course, had already sprinted after his target, who darted between the houses to avoid the circle of sage, heading for the seafront instead.

I ran in that direction and found that Maurice had skidded to a halt on the cliff's edge. "She jumped into the water."

"She didn't, did she?" I looked down, seeing a head bobbing in the water. "She's lucky she missed the rocks."

"Is the demon still possessing her?" Callum caught up to us. "No way to tell from up here, I guess."

"Possessed or not, I'm not getting her out of there," said Maurice.

"Right." Callum swore under his breath. Then he shifted into a giant wolf and leapt over the cliff's edge.

"Hey!" Maurice's alarmed shout prompted hurried footsteps to rise behind us, but our attention was riveted on the water. Callum's furry head emerged from the waves, and he began swimming towards the witch's retreating figure.

"He's lucky he didn't hit those rocks too," I breathed. "The fur probably helps..."

"That's no excuse." Maurice had gone chalk white. "Can't you levitate them out of there?"

"I can."

The waves made it tricky to aim, but werewolves were strong swimmers when they wanted to be. In seconds, Callum had heaved the witch's body out of the water, onto the rocks below. He then grabbed her by the scruff of her neck in his jaws and began to climb.

I became conscious of the murmurs of panic from the crowd behind me, but Callum didn't acknowledge them. He clambered into view, spraying everyone with seawater, and the crowd parted when he ran straight through them with the witch's limp body still dangling from his mouth.

Swiftly, I moved to follow, and I caught up when Callum dropped the witch into the circle of sage. The witch doubled over, coughing, and then lifted her head. A familiar blackness oozed out of her chest as the creature relinquished its grip on her.

I raised my wand and cast a banishment spell, which hit the demonic spirit head-on. Light suffused the circle, and when it cleared, the creature was gone.

"Two down, however many to go." I glanced down at the witch, who'd lifted her head in confusion.

"Scarlet?" she asked in a high, panicky voice. "What's going on?"

"You were possessed." I looked at Maurice. "Are there any others?"

"That," said Maurice, "is a very good question. I can't tell."

Callum growled, still in wolf form, and the same growl was echoed by the chimera. Lara came back into view, gripping Cupcake's lead.

"He's really riled up," she said. "Cupcake, can you make some noise? See if we can scare out any more hiding demons?"

The chimera tried to hide behind Lara, who sighed. "Sorry. I don't think he's going to—"

Callum reared up on his hind legs and roared. Everyone jumped, but no more flat black eyes appeared amid their ranks. Nearly every villager had assembled outside by this point, even Charles, but there was one face missing from among their number.

Backing to Tam's side, I whispered, "Did you see where Walter went?"

He frowned. "No, I didn't."

"I did." Maurice's gaze snapped up, and he pointed through a gap in the houses. "He went that way."

He zipped out of sight and returned an instant later with an indignant Walter in tow. "How dare you manhandle me? This is the second time you've assaulted me, and I won't stand for it."

Cupcake growled, low and menacing, and lunged forward in a sudden motion that dragged Lara behind him. Before any of us could blink, the chimera had Walter pinned down beneath one leonine paw.

"Is he possessed?" Maurice bared his fangs. "I knew there was something off about this guy."

"I am *not* possessed," Walter said, his voice high and panicky.

"He isn't," said Farley, "but he's feeling awfully guilty for something."

"You're the summoner," I said to Walter. "Aren't you?"

"I am not." He whimpered when the chimera's paw pressed against his chest. "I am ... I didn't mean for anyone to get killed."

"You're the summoner?" Scarlet stepped over to him, making sure to put at least a little distance between herself and the chimera. "You summoned those abominations?"

"He is," said Maurice. "I can't read all his thoughts, but I can see enough."

Walter let out a sad moan. "Nobody was supposed to get hurt. I was trying to protect us."

"Fenton's death is on your hands," said Scarlet. "You don't deny having him killed."

Walter whimpered again. "Fenton... He must have guessed Charles was possessed and confronted him, which forced the demon to react in its own defence."

My hands fisted. "You can't be surprised when demons do whatever they want. That's why it's illegal to summon them."

"Speaking of which," said Tam, "how many exactly did you summon?"

He squeezed his eyes shut. "Three. Only three."

"That means we're missing one."

We might have found our summoner, but the fight wasn't over yet.

15

After Walter's confession, Scarlet wasted no time in hauling him off to jail. At least she'd finally arrested the right person, but her coven members continued to watch our group with suspicion. The fact that Callum was still in wolf form didn't help, nor that Cupcake remained close at hand, growling under his breath. I scanned the other villagers for any signs of flat black eyes, but I didn't see any.

I turned to Maurice and lowered my voice. "Can you read their minds?"

His forehead screwed up. "A little. Yeah. It's coming back."

"Oh good." Farley's shoulders slumped with relief. "Nice improvisation, Callum."

In a flash of fur, Callum transformed back into a human. "I don't like scaring people, but I didn't have any better ideas."

"We had to lure the demons out into the open." I belatedly noticed the state of Callum's clothes, which hung off his body in rags from when they'd torn as he'd shifted into a wolf. "Did you pack any spare clothes?"

"No." Callum shivered. "This is why I don't usually shift on missions."

I caught sight of Maurice, whose flushed face was even more noticeable on a vampire than on a human. Tam, however, didn't appear to have noticed. He'd crouched next to the circle of sage, wearing a frown. When he saw me looking, he lifted his head. "There were only two demons here?"

"No—Walter said three," I said. "The other must be hiding."

Farley shook her head. "It's not over."

The villagers seemed to think it was, though. Some of them had begun to return to their houses, while others followed Scarlet back to the witches' headquarters. I hoped she'd let Charles out of jail now she had the real culprit. And Alana, too, though she'd also committed the supposed crime of concealing her vampire status from the rest of the coven. Even if she was allowed out of jail, her coven might not let her escape without punishment. Perhaps that was why our victory felt so uncertain. There was still a stack of unanswered questions awaiting us back in Herring Cove.

Cupcake whined, and I turned to his owner. "Is he okay?"

"He's uncertain about being around so many people."

"I can relate," Farley said wryly. "Are we going to leave the sage here?"

"I think we should." Tam straightened upright and took a step back from the circle of sage. "In case any more spirits reveal themselves."

"Do you think it's likely?" There it was again—a nagging doubt, the certainty that we'd missed something vital. Yes,

Grim Crag was no less creepy without a couple of demons hiding among the villagers, but what about the third?

My phone buzzed in my pocket. Kellen was asking for an update. I hesitated, on the brink of telling him we'd dealt with the demons, but he had his own battle on his hands with the upper echelons of the Wardens who'd sent the inspector.

I lowered my hand and addressed Tam. "We're going back to Herring Cove?"

He inclined his head. "Unless you want to wait to speak to Scarlet again."

"I'd like to see Alana set free, but..."

Another growl came from the chimera.

"We left a mess behind us that we ought to clean up."

"Oh, fun." Farley pulled a face. "Our delightful inspector will be waiting with another lecture. What'll he say when we tell him we caught the demons?"

"Probably that we broke all the rules," Callum said through chattering teeth. "Want to get it over with?"

"Yes, preferably before you freeze to death," said Farley. "Tam?"

"If you're all sure." He began to walk away from the village.

Maurice overtook us in seconds, though he didn't move at quite his usual speed. Reluctant to go back to face the inspector's wrath, I guessed.

I fell into step with Tam as we walked. "Kellen asked for an update. He didn't say whether he's managed to find anyone willing to back us up against the inspector yet."

"He might have some difficulty finding anyone to come here in person," he said. "This place is remote enough that it's no wonder we were assigned the only inspector in the area."

The nagging doubt inside me intensified. "The only inspector in the area, who was already looking for monsters."

"Yes." He tilted his head. "What is it, Perry?"

I took in a deep breath. "I might be mistaken, but I think the inspector is possessed as well."

Tam studied me for several moments. "The inspector? You think so?"

"It would explain why he completely dropped the ball on his actual mission." I shook my head. "Lara said he started out perfectly reasonable and then veered sideways into being completely irrational. And what *did* happen to her chimera licence?"

"What about Cupcake?" asked Lara, overhearing.

"Would you say the inspector almost seemed like a different person when you first interacted with him compared to how he is now?"

"I'd say yes," she said. "I couldn't put it into words before, but that's how it seemed."

"What do you mean?" asked Farley.

I raised my voice a little so the others could hear. "I think he might be possessed as well."

"The inspector?" Callum grimaced. "I knew there was something off about the guy."

Farley's face paled. "You can't be serious. He's possessed?"

"Who's possessed?" Maurice backed up a few steps, slowing his pace so he could hear us.

"The inspector," I said. "If nothing else, it explains why he's going out of his way to sabotage our attempts to solve the murders."

Farley swore. "If you're right, what are we supposed to do?"

"Corner him and dump a ton of sage on his head?" I suggested.

Callum snorted. "We don't have *that* much sage left, but why'd he ask us to come here if he didn't want us to catch him out?"

"It was the Wardens who sent out the orders," I said. "No wonder he was so ticked off at being asked to assess us. Though Kellen is going to have trouble finding any dirt on him in the Wardens' records."

"Damn, you're right," said Farley. "He was probably a normal guy before he got himself possessed."

"I guarantee that dude has never been normal in his life," Maurice said. "And for the record, you might be right. I couldn't always read his thoughts, but I assumed it was because he'd had training to keep vampires out."

"You didn't mention that before," Callum said. "Didn't that strike you as weird?"

He shrugged. "He's not the first inspector who hasn't been a fan of our team ... especially some of us."

My eye twitched. "I'd be the first to admit that's true, but some of the stuff he said to me was out of order. He seemed more interested in getting under my skin than actually assessing me."

"I got that impression too," Callum said. "I thought he was just angry about our lack of progress in solving the murders."

So had I, and I'd never thought that he might be possessed by one of the demons who'd killed three people. The question was 'How could we lure him out?' I assumed the usual rules against assaulting our fellow Wardens would fly out the window when the Warden in question was possessed, though I ought to get confirmation from Tam before I did anything rash.

The team leader had gone quiet, his expression preoccupied, as if he was thinking over our options.

"Tam," I said. "What happens when a Warden goes rogue? What's the procedure?"

"We'll worry about that later," said Tam. "We need to get to him before he realises we're aware of the demon, because if it feels threatened, it might escape or even hide itself within another host."

"I don't see it letting him go that easily." *Not with the power of authority the inspector wields.* The demon had chosen its host well.

Had we ever really been talking to Inspector Peterson at all or simply a demon wearing his face? I couldn't be sure, but while part of me hoped we'd run into him on the way back to Herring Cove again, he was nowhere to be seen.

"Where is he?" Callum muttered as we neared Herring Cove. "I didn't think he'd stand for us locking him up."

"I hope *he* hasn't called the office," I said. "Or got the police in on his schemes as well."

"Don't tell me they're possessed too." Farley groaned.

When we reached the path leading into the village, Cupcake came to a halt and began to growl.

"Not again." Lara tugged on his lead, but he refused to budge. "He might sense the demon. Do you want me to bring him to the inn?"

"Not sure we'll find the inspector there." I thought. "Should we check in with the police first?"

"I can't exactly walk in there like this," Callum said dryly. "Anyone else want to volunteer?"

"I would," said Tam, "but I did tell you we aren't splitting up."

A tense silence ensued. We all knew what was at stake. The last time the team had split up when facing a demon, it had ended in tragedy. The inspector knew, too, and so did the demon. It wouldn't surprise me if he'd taken it into account when he'd planned this mission.

He'd used the team's history against us … but perhaps I could do the same for him.

"I'll talk to him alone," I offered. "I'm the one he has the biggest grudge against, so I can divert his attention while the rest of you lay a trap for the demon."

"You can't be serious," said Callum. "We're not leaving you alone with that guy. *Or* the demon."

"The demon won't try to possess me." I tried to inject as much certainty as possible into my tone. "Besides, I've been wanting to punch the guy in the face for a while."

"I'm all in favour of sneaking up on him from behind while Perry has him distracted," Maurice ventured. "You guys can set up another circle of sage, can't you?"

"I guess," Farley said doubtfully. "Perry, are you sure you want to do this?"

"I'm sure." My gaze connected with Tam's. I saw a mixture of concern and admiration. Warmth spread through my entire body. My team leader had faith in me, and that was enough. "Put what's left of the sage in a circle, and I'll lure out the demon."

Tam inclined his head. "Do as she says."

As the others moved to obey, I approached the inn. My heart raced as I reached for the door and pushed it inward.

Nobody was in the lobby—not the inspector or the inn's owners. The door to the dining room lay ajar, and nobody appeared to be in there either. I ducked inside and jumped out of my skin when the inn's owner emerged from the back room.

"Looking for that inspector?" She pursed her lips. "He left not long after you did. Went to the police station."

"He's possessed by a demon." Was she? I really couldn't tell, but the reminder that Tam had planned to check in with the police nudged its way to the front of my mind. "If I were you, I'd stay hidden out of sight until this is over."

Without waiting for a reply, I hurried outside. The door to the police station opened a second later, and the inspector walked out.

"You." Inspector Peterson caught sight of me. "You're back. I assume your mission was a success?"

"Almost." My heart thudded against my ribcage as I faced the inspector. "You didn't think we wouldn't find you out, did you?"

His expression showed nothing but polite incredulity. "What on earth are you talking about?"

"You almost had me fooled, you know," I said. "Where's Tam?"

Please say he didn't go into the station. He could hold his own in a fight, but against a demon? I didn't want to find that one out the hard way.

"I haven't the faintest idea," he said. "Shouldn't *you* know where your team leader is?"

"He sent me to do this alone," I lied. "After all, I'm the one you really have an issue with, aren't I? Both you and the demon."

A muscle ticked in his jaw. "Your team will answer for what you did to me earlier. I don't care for your reasoning—it's against the code of the Wardens to assault a superior officer."

"Speaking of officers, where are the police?" I peered through the window of the police office, which was cast in darkness. "Why were you in their office?"

"They decided to take the rest of the day off."

"You didn't answer the second question." I raised my

wand. "What were you doing in there? Doctoring more records or hiding paperwork like the chimera licence?"

His expression flattened. "You should have left the Wardens of your own accord."

"What *is* your problem with me?"

This couldn't be just about me, surely. Even if the inspector did have a personal grudge against me, and the demonic spirit had fed on that hate and warped it beyond all recognition, it didn't explain why he'd picked our team, of all possible options. I couldn't be the only person the inspector disliked, surely.

Unless... Did the *demon* know me too?

Inspector Peterson's mouth twisted, and he pulled out his wand. "You're a disgrace to the Wardens. They should never have let in someone who harbours a curse."

"Is being cursed worse than being possessed by a demon?" I challenged him. "Also, I was asking the demon. There's no reason for a spirit to care about my being cursed."

"I beg to differ." A familiar flat blackness entered his eyes, and his voice dropped to a mutter. "You truly want to know why we despise you, Perry Jacobs? You've banished enough of us from this realm that I would have thought it would be obvious."

"It's my job to banish demons." I wasn't the only Warden with that particular skillset, so it still didn't explain why he'd singled out my team. "Part of my duty as a Warden is to rid the world of creatures like you. I'm hardly unique."

"You're mistaken." He raised his wand, pointing it directly at me. "You're too dangerous to be left unchallenged."

"Unchallenged? I banished another of your sort only last week." I pointed my wand right back at him, ready to deflect whatever spell he flung at me. "You seemed more interested in talking to me about the team's history. Were you acquainted with *that* demon?"

"Yes." His voice dropped to a guttural growl. "I'm glad he was able to take one of your team down with him."

Fury surged within me. I waved my wand, but he was prepared. Smoke swirled from the inspector's hands, deflecting my spell straight back at me. I dropped to the ground, my knockback spell whistling over my head, and he stalked towards me.

"Your team will be sorry they let you into their ranks."

"No!" Farley shouted from the street's end. "We won't."

Farley. I hadn't intended for the others to show themselves yet, but a cruel smile twisted the demon's mouth when he saw her.

"You," he said. "How I wish I'd been there to taste your despair on the day your teammate died."

Farley choked on a sob, but she held her ground. "You don't stand a chance against all of us. Where is Tam?"

Good question. He *hadn't* been inside the police station, had he? If so ... no. Tam was resourceful enough that he wouldn't have been so easily thwarted.

The demon smiled. "I put him down."

An icy sensation plunged to my core. "You're lying."

"No!" The cry came from Maurice, who slammed into the inspector from behind with all his vampire strength.

Callum, back in the form of a wolf, leapt over to join in. The demon hissed, faced with two opponents at once, and I seized the chance to raise my wand again. My next spell hit him square in the chest, sending him staggering back a step.

The inspector gave a strangled laugh. "You won't detach me from my host that easily. I've grown fond of him."

"You're just as twisted as each other," Farley said, her own wand in her hand. "But you're outnumbered."

Callum and Maurice both pounced, driving the inspector backwards. That was when I spotted the sage sprinkled in a line near the end of the street, waiting to entrap the demon.

"Get out!" I cast another spell that sent him tumbling head over heels, but when he came upright in the circle of sage, the blackness didn't leave his eyes. The demon wasn't kidding about being attached to its host—but how to remove it without killing the inspector and condemning ourselves in the process?

The demon laughed. "This is futile. No mere circle can keep me contained."

"I disagree." Tam appeared behind him, his face bloodied, but he was very much alive. He raised his stick-like weapon in both hands, then he swung it at the inspector's head.

A thud, and the inspector crumpled into a heap. Blackness arose, detaching itself from his body.

"That ought to do it," Tam said. "Perry?"

My instincts pushed through my shock, driving me to raise my wand. "I banish you from this world, demon."

Farley raised her wand, too, and our spells collided with the inspector at the same instant. Light illuminated the darkness, which emitted a deafening howl before vanishing into nothingness.

"It's gone." Farley's voice was hoarse. "We did it."

We had, but I couldn't seem to look away from Tam. "He... He said he killed you."

"I'm hard to kill," said Tam. "So is he, I hope, because someone's going to have to question the inspector when he wakes up."

"Good point." With difficulty, I dragged my gaze away to look at the others—including Lara, who'd arrived with a reluctant chimera in tow. "So ... who's going to call the Wardens?"

16

———

Several hectic minutes later, we had the inspector securely locked up in the inn's kitchen—the smallest available room. Tam had a nasty cut on the top of his head that needed seeing to, though he insisted he was fine, while Callum disappeared upstairs to change into clothes that weren't torn. Farley offered to explain the situation to the inn's bewildered owners, who'd at least handed over the key to the kitchen without raising a fuss. No doubt the knowledge that they'd unknowingly harboured a demon under their roof for days had helped, though that left it to Maurice or me to call the Wardens' office and explain everything.

"You call them," the vampire said. "I'll check up on the police. They might be at home, oblivious to all this, but I wouldn't put anything past that demon."

"Guess not." I retrieved my phone from my pocket and walked out of the inn. "Here goes nothing."

Once again, Kellen answered my call right away. "Perry. Are you all right?"

"Yeah." I closed the inn's door behind me. "We dealt with

all three demons. The slight issue is that one of them was possessing the inspector. He's currently locked up at the inn."

A faint groan came from his end. "I suspected something was amiss, but I hoped I was wrong."

"Yeah … it took a while for us to work it out," I said. "I'm pretty sure he was conscious for at least some of the time he was possessed, so it's hard to say how many of the decisions were his and how many were the demon's."

He gave another groan. "This is going to create a hell of a lot of paperwork."

"Not for you, surely," I said. "You aren't *his* supervisor."

"I'm your supervisor—all of you—and it's up to me to ensure the Wardens get the full story of what happened over there in Herring Cove." He exhaled a sigh. "The fact that the inspector turned out to be under the influence of a demon will sway the case in your favour, make no mistake, but if the man himself was involved in any of the decisions he made … it'll be hard to prove."

I gripped the phone. "You're saying it's my word against his, then? I have to talk to upper management?"

"If necessary, yes."

I closed my eyes. "Do you know what he said to me in the end? He said the Wardens thought my curse was a risk from the start, and I should never have signed up. Even the *demon* thought I was too dangerous to be allowed to live."

A pause followed. "That's not true, Perry."

But some of the Wardens *did* strongly dislike me. That was no secret, and if they measured my word against Inspector Peterson's, would my record win out over his? I doubted it.

"True or not, who's likely to take the fall?" I queried. "I defied his orders several times, long before we knew he was possessed, and if he'd been allowed to have his way, I'd have been kicked off the team, at the very least. If not expelled from the Wardens as a whole."

"That won't happen." Certainty suffused his tone. "I promised to vouch for you at every step, and that won't change."

My eyes stung. "Even if upper management wants me gone?"

"They won't," he said. "The rest of the team will be interviewed, too, and they'll be able to back you up."

"Not soon, I hope. Our team leader took a blow to the head when the inspector tried to kill him."

He sucked in a breath. "I'll see what I can do."

Kellen ended the call with the promise that the Wardens' office would send someone in to collect the inspector by morning, but I didn't hold out much hope that he'd remain unconscious until then. It was probably better that he didn't, because that would mean he'd suffered long-term brain damage, making it even harder to prove he'd been partially in control of his actions while the demon had been possessing him.

When I returned to the inn, I found Tam pacing back and forth at the foot of the stairs. While Callum had had to more or less drag Tam upstairs to fetch the team's first aid kit and see to his wound, he still hadn't cleaned the blood off his face. It ought to have made him look a mess, but instead it gave him an aura of dangerousness that I'd be lying if I said I didn't find more than a little attractive.

"Kellen said a team's on the way to collect the inspector," I told him. "Where are the others?"

"In here." Farley ducked out of the dining room. "He's awake. The inspector is. Seems to be in control of his mental functions too."

"More's the pity." Callum came downstairs, having changed out of his torn clothes. "Where's Maurice?"

"Here." The vampire slipped out of the dining room behind Farley, an expression of distaste on his face. When I caught him eyeing Tam's wound, I guessed the sight of the blood had no doubt tripped his vampire instincts.

"If the inspector's awake, it's good news for us," I said to general surprise from everyone except Tam. "If he's able to give a coherent recollection of the past few days, then it's more likely that the Wardens will believe our claims that the demon wasn't always in the driver's seat."

"Exactly," said Tam. "When will Kellen's team get here?"

"By morning, he said." At the thought of what else he'd said, my heart began to beat faster. "And ... he said we'll have to speak to the higher-ups ourselves. Not yet but soon. It's the only way to see to it that Inspector Peterson isn't allowed to walk free."

"How's it likely to play out for us?" Callum asked Tam.

"With a little luck, he'll be arrested for conspiring with demons, and we'll walk away free," I said. I didn't add that luck was something I was usually short on, but the scepticism in Maurice's expression suggested he'd guessed my line of thinking. Unless he'd actually read my mind—which, if it meant the inn was now a demon-free zone, didn't bother me nearly as much as it normally would.

Tam caught my eye, and the calmness in his gaze soothed my racing nerves a little. "Then we'll hope for that."

"We can ask those lazy police officers to back us up," Maurice said. "They've been at home the whole time. Would you believe it?"

"I suspected that must be the case," said Tam. "I'm glad nobody else was hurt."

"Lucky we were the targets." The inn's owners had had a

fortunate escape. That was for sure. I spotted the woman lurking out of sight in the dining room, her gaze fixed on the closed door behind which the inspector was locked up.

"He's not trying to escape, is he?" I asked her.

"No, but I can't cook with him locked up in my kitchen. What're we to do for dinner?"

"Hmm." Come to think of it, I was starving. "Anyone want to call for takeout?"

"Yes," Callum answered. "What're our options?"

"Fish and chips, probably." Farley dropped her voice so the inn's owner wouldn't overhear. "No more fish. I'll stick with the chips."

"Same here."

I'd had enough of the smell of fish for a lifetime.

THE WARDENS' team showed up just before dawn. A middle-aged ogre entered the lobby first, surveying our bedraggled group, and two other ogres followed him. They made a menacing sight, and I didn't blame the inn's owners for backing into the dining room.

"You're the team who called us here?" asked the first ogre.

"That's us." Tam, who'd finally cleaned the blood from his face, beckoned him into the dining room. "The inspector is secured in the inn's kitchen. He's no longer possessed, but he might be a danger to himself and others all the same."

"Possessed," the ogre repeated, his tusks twisting his mouth into a grimace. "Never would have believed it if Kellen hadn't told me."

A wary sense of hope arose inside me. Most of the ogres in the department were friends with one another, so Kellen must have picked out a team who were more likely to give us an easier time.

"It took a while for us to figure it out, but by then, it was almost too late. He was acting like himself until the very end, when he attacked our team leader."

"Kellen mentioned you think he was consciously allying with the demon," he grunted. "Hard to prove, but we'll take him into custody for his own safety as well as yours."

"Thank you," said Tam. "He's currently unarmed, but I'd still be careful."

The ogre lumbered through the dining room to the kitchen, where the inn's terrified owner handed over the key. As the door opened, the inspector looked imploringly up at the ogre. "I'm being held against my will!"

"On the orders of the higher Wardens, you're to come with us," said the ogre. "You can come peacefully or face arrest. Your choice."

Inspector Peterson rose shakily to his feet. "This is an outrage. These individuals attacked a superior officer, but you think *I* should be punished?"

"We have evidence enough that you broke a large number of our rules in your handling of the chimera case," the ogre growled. "When added to your clear attempts to thwart Tam's team's investigation into the tragic murders of two tourists, it doesn't look good for you."

"I was following procedures," he said stiffly. "Even if they refused to."

"You'll have the chance to explain yourself in your trial," one of the other ogres told him. "Come on now."

Ha. I suppressed a grin as the inspector strode out of the room, and the ogres flanked him on either side, escorting him out of the inn.

The leading ogre remained behind to address Tam. "I

will be in touch with you shortly. For now, you should return to your base."

"Of course," said Tam. "Give us a few hours to settle things with the authorities here, and we'll head straight back."

I was in dire need of a nap, but we did have a few loose ends to tie up, starting with Grim Crag. After we'd packed up our belongings following a thoroughly sleepless night, we left the inn for the other village.

I didn't expect a warm welcome from Scarlet, but neither did anyone try to chase us off when we reached the cluster of houses on the clifftop. My attention went to Alana's house first, whose door lay slightly ajar. Hoping Scarlet hadn't repurposed her house in her absence, I inched closer to the door and startled when Alana herself appeared in the doorway with the stealthy speed of a vampire. "Oh, it's you."

"Scarlet let you go?"

She inclined her head. "Yes, but I have to vacate my house and leave the community at once."

"That's unjust," said Farley. "She can't kick you out."

"She can, and to be honest, I don't *want* to stay," she said. "I don't suppose you can recommend a hotel?"

"Er ... I wouldn't necessarily recommend the inn we stayed at in Herring Cove, but it's all I know." I glanced at the others, who shrugged, not knowing any better options either. "Though if you come to Herring Cove, I can ask Lara to meet you there. She might have another recommendation. She's the witch with the pet chimera."

"You're joking, aren't you?" she asked. "I'm not going near that thing."

"Lara is nice enough," I said. "I think she'd be willing to help you out. She saw for herself how uncompromising Scarlet can be."

Her shoulders slumped. "She's not *all* bad, though. She let Charles off the hook, though the poor guy is still devastated over Fenton's death. She just took issue with me for being, well, undead."

"Being a vampire has its perks." Maurice bared his fangs at her in what I assumed was supposed to be a show of solidarity. "You don't need that coven."

She cast a glance over at the coven's headquarters and gave a faint sigh. "I don't have much to lose, at this point."

"I'll let Lara know you might drop by Herring Cove." I turned to the others. "You know what? I don't think Scarlet deserves a visit from us. If she wants an explanation, she can come to Herring Cove herself."

Visiting the coven would result in us being surrounded by a flood of ungrateful coven members who wouldn't have a word of thanks to offer, and who'd voted to chase off one of their own people. I had little sympathy for Scarlet at this stage.

"I can't say I'm keen to see her," Farley ventured. "She gives me a headache, frankly."

"Same here, and I'm not even an empath," added Callum. "Though if she *does* drop by Herring Cove, I hope she won't bother Lara or her chimera."

"I think they'll be fine." I began to walk away from Alana's house. "I also think we can convince Lara to help Alana. Her chimera is practically nocturnal, which helps."

"But does Alana want to stay with a chimera?" Farley asked.

"There are worse things to have as a roommate." *Such as a demon sharing one's body, for instance.*

"Like spiders?" Callum asked lightly.

"Don't even." I caught sight of Maurice smirking and shot him a warning look, though I'd happily deal with the spiders if it meant we got to return to the tower as soon as possible.

Back at Herring Cove, we went to the inn to fetch our luggage before dropping in at Lara's house. As I'd predicted, she reacted with indignation to Alana's plight.

"I can't believe that Scarlet kicked her out of her home for being a vampire," she said. "I'd be happy to help her get back on her feet while she figures out where to go."

"Thanks," I said. "You know ... we never did pay her back for borrowing her sage."

"I'm pretty sure she'll understand," said Lara. "I'll tell her. If I don't see you around again, then I hope you have a safe trip home."

As we left her house, Maurice asked, "If we're going back to the tower, does someone else get to pick the mode of transport this time around?"

"Up to you," I said. "Want to fly?"

"Definitely not," said Callum.

"Agreed," said Farley.

"She dropped me in the sea!" Maurice objected.

"There's no sea near the tower," I pointed out. "Besides, don't you want to go back home?"

Home. I'd never used that word to refer to the tower before, but it came out as naturally as breathing. I found my gaze drawn to Tam's, and my insides warmed at his smile. This, I was sure, was worth the risk.

When Maurice sighed and didn't argue, I raised my wand, and Herring Cove vanished, to be replaced by the gravel path outside the tower.

I'd never been so happy to see the castle's grey stone walls or to smell the forest's woodsy smell in place of the stench of fish. Even the birds sounded happy to see us— until Maurice yelled, "You'll pay for that!"

The vampire had landed in a deep puddle that covered the end of the path that bordered the forest. *Oops.*

"I didn't do that on purpose," I told him.

"The hell you didn't. That's twice now."

I rolled my eyes. "Look, it's been raining. Puddles aren't exactly an uncommon thing around here."

He spluttered in outrage, and I heard Tam laughing behind me. My heart rose in response, despite my knowledge of the battle still to come. The demons knew my name, and the Wardens had me on their watchlist ... but I knew that the others would have my back.

The tower was my home, and I'd fight to keep it with everything I had.

ABOUT THE AUTHOR

Elle Adams lives in the middle of England, where she spends most of her time reading an ever-growing mountain of books, planning her next adventure, or writing. Elle's books are humorous mysteries with a paranormal twist, packed with magical mayhem.

She also writes urban and contemporary fantasy novels as Emma L. Adams.

Visit http://www.elleadamsauthor.com/ to find out more about Elle's books.